LAST WORDS ON EARTH

JAVIER SERENA

Translated from the Spanish
by Katie Whittemore

OPEN LETTER

LITERARY TRANSLATIONS FROM THE UNIVERSITY OF ROCHESTER

LAST WORDS ON EARTH

I

I'LL CALL HIM RICARDO, Ricardo Funes, although that isn't his real first name, or last. I won't reveal any factual details about him, except to say that he was from Peru and never forgot that he was an exile, not even after three whole decades in Spain.

Funes resided in Spain for thirty years: in Barcelona, at first, and then other Catalan towns during his nomadic phase, in which he devoted himself to selling leather goods at flea markets, repairing watches, and performing stints as a night watchman at various campgrounds, until finally settling in Lloret de Mar.

Now that statues have been built in his honor and he is universally admired after his untimely death, Funes the man has been obscured by the towering shadow of his legend, his history appropriated and fetishized, his works quoted and beloved by all. But his literary triumph couldn't have seemed more unlikely when I first met him, when he was just a poor, twenty-something immigrant silenced on the margins. A true outcast.

That's what I thought that first day: here was a lunatic or hermit, a pariah forced to live on the village outskirts. I've never forgotten the impression he made. I met Funes at the invitation of a mutual friend, a fellow writer who taught at the Universitat de Girona and had discovered Funes the previous summer at a campground near the coastal town of Castelldefels, where Ricardo Funes's mother temporarily set up a notions shop, selling bits and bobs until the day she decamped for yet another inland town, driven by the habitual, ingrained nomadism that defined their little family of two. I decided to accompany my professor friend to Castelldefels after several phone conversations during which he described Funes with an intriguing mix of skepticism and appeal. According to my friend, Funes was more familiar with certain periods of Latin American literature than even some of his department colleagues, but the man expressed himself with declarations so provocative it proved impossible to invite him to give a lecture. "It's like he has to argue until the other person is offended," he said, explaining that Funes had recently been fired from the campground because, while an inebriated English vacationer almost drowned in the pool, Funes was reading instead of making his nightly rounds. Finding himself without a job and with a bit of money, Funes had apparently decided to spend all his savings on a shack near the beach rather than follow his mother out of town.

I had heard so much about him from my friend that I decided I would join him on a trek out to Funes's hut. The May day was so cold and rain-swept that it seemed to exaggerate Funes's status as an exiled resistance fighter living in poverty. It's strange to think how forsaken he was back then given the commotion caused, decades later, by any old manuscript found on his computer. But back in those days, Ricardo Funes was so far removed from ordinary life that he was characterized as somewhat of an outlaw who harried the other villagers: "Watch yourselves now, the Peruvian's mutt probably hasn't eaten in awhile," a neighbor advised us, peering out from under the hood of his raincoat when we stopped to check our directions.

Such a warning would later prove unnecessary, as I never sensed even the slightest hint of a threat in any of Funes's gestures, not that day nor in any of the years to come. It did, however, serve to amplify the mysteriousness of the scene in which we found ourselves. After the neighbor's ominous words, we pressed on down the dirt road for several minutes, through tree boughs clawing the windshield and muddy patches where our tires spun, until we finally reached an empty clearing.

And there, for the first time, I was met with Ricardo Funes's extraordinary presence. I saw him from the car, a hundred meters away, planted in front of the house like a sentinel guarding his homestead in the Old West. The shack was a rustic, single-story construction with a haphazard tin roof, and Funes stood outside with his dog, clutching not a shotgun, but a stick, surrounded by shirts and pairs of pants strung on a line, flapping like flags in the breeze.

We got out of the car, and as my friend and I walked toward him, I sensed his endearing amiability, which I would come to know as one of Funes's characteristic qualities. He donned a summer shirt with green and orange flowers, more appropriate for Caribbean isles than our European latitudes. His hair was long and curly and he wore the round metal-framed glasses he would favor until he died. Rounding out his general appearance as a stray tourist-cum-novice farmer were a pair of sandals entirely ineffectual at protecting his bare feet from the mud.

"Welcome, professor." Funes greeted my friend ironically, shaking his hand with sincere affection.

Then he turned to me. I took in his open shirt, unbuttoned to reveal a patch of chest hair and a silver chain. He was thin as a greyhound and in his unmistakable, hoarse voice—perpetual rumble, incurable lament—addressed me in a way that immediately won me over:

"And you are also very welcome, señor Vallés, sir," he joked. "I've read all of your books."

In time, I would come to learn that two of Funes's most emblematic behaviors were to read everything and declare it publicly, and to express his opinions—whatever they were—with total sincerity and no reservation whatsoever,

6

devoid of any strategy to advance his own interests. Pretense was not to be found among his defects.

That afternoon, however, I was less taken with his literary reflections than with the spectacle of neglect in which he lived.

The house struck me as so chaotic, so unsuitable for habitation, that it was a wonder he had already been living there for months. The first jolt was the strong smell permeating the place: the odor of a closed, musty pantry, or of the thick air of an unaired bedroom. It smelled as though Funes lived on nicotine and caffeine and wore his clothes so many times in a row that he didn't remember how to wash them to expunge the pervasive stench.

In the main living area—the only room besides the bedroom—there was a kitchenette and sink piled high with plates and pots and pans, a couch covered in an array of blankets, clothing strewn across the floor, and books stacked in towers on shelves and atop the television. My friend and I sat down at a small table pushed against the wall that appeared to be used both for eating and working at his typewriter.

We sat quietly, taken aback by the shambolic state of his quarters, as he showed us the folders where he kept his manuscripts organized by year and genre—poetry, short story, or novel—in a meticulous color-coded filing system completely at odds with the rest of the house.

"Your first book is your best," he said, crossing his legs and establishing the candidness that would govern the terms of our future friendship. He lit his first cigarette before my friend or I had even ventured to try the coffee he offered.

The rest of the conversation unfolded along those lines, a succession of erudite comments and rash declarations. Funes didn't hesitate to show contempt for acclaimed writers or extol the virtues of others we hadn't even heard of, all with a confidence in his own judgment that I had rarely seen in anyone else. "His writing will be completely outmoded before you know it," he said about a popular prize-winning novelist. Or, in reference to a poet he had always admired who lived as a recluse: "He's one of two or three who will actually last," calming his dog with a pat. The animal hadn't stopped yipping, whining, and sniffing our legs under the table.

The situation was an ironic one, since by that time I had already published several books and had a weekly column in *La Vanguardia*, as befit the profile of the sort of writer I represented, vaguely bohemian but from a well-to-do Barcelonan family, and my beguiled professor friend balanced his own writing with teaching at the university in Girona, and yet here was this man, tucked away in a peasant's shack, lecturing us with his strident, melodramatic opinions.

Eventually, the professor redirected the conversation toward more exotic subjects: he asked Funes to tell me about *negacionismo*, a poetic movement Funes had apparently founded as an adolescent in Mexico, where he went into exile during the Peruvian dictatorship. The movement's literary tendencies embraced a puzzling appetite for

8

rebellion: Funes claimed to have sabotaged readings given by the most renowned poets of the day and published irreverent pamphlets railing against the dominant national canon.

Funes drained his black coffee in a single swallow and lit a second cigarette using the first; behind his thin lips, I noted the teeth destroyed by lack of oral hygiene and many years of dental neglect. As he started to speak, his eyes shone. He was abidingly proud of his turbulent teen-age years.

He spoke enthusiastically about the magazines he published with his handful of co-conspirators, and evoked the years that immediately preceded his departure for Barcelona: vibrant days of his youth in Mexico City, an adolescence in which he must have felt that the city streets had been paved expressly for him to roam at dawn with his silhouette shining nobly, unstained by disappointment; a time when he yearned to wield language as a tool for destroying all the barriers built with apathy and all the traditions he wanted to shatter.

By then, the room was filled with smoke—tobacco smoke and the turgidity from the conversation, which had become a monologue, replete with names of streets and old Mexican associates and obscure books of poetry. While outside the rain fell with increasing force, inside intimacy reigned, accentuated by the sound of the raindrops patter-ing on the metal roof.

Funes waxed poetic about his minor feats, reminisc-ing about his years of excess and even alluding to the punishments meted out when a member crossed over to the ranks of the powerful, punishments that called to mind the rituals of masonic sects or other insurgent cabals. After a brief pause, he reached for a knife stuck through a newspaper clipping into the wall, pulled the weapon out, and viciously stabbed the same piece of paper again.

"Traitor! Sold. For a chair and an office." He explained that the figures in the photo were an old *negacionista* comrade and a powerful literary critic, one who had apparently taken the poet under his protection for some future gain.

Between threats directed at the man in the picture, Funes detailed the scope of the knife-pierced individual's unforgivable sin: that of putting his own future before his loyalty to the group, of abandoning his tribe of aspiring-poet friends who read each other's scrawled verses, all in exchange for an institutional fellowship, or inclusion in some anthology. There was no graver offense in Ricardo Funes's mind, as I would observe over and again throughout the years. He clung to that peculiar poetic cause sparked in the Americas and protected its distant flame like it was his only source of warmth, the final thread connecting him to his origins.

Present in those accounts was his closest friend from his Mexico days, Domingo Pasquiano, whom I would never have the chance to meet, although Funes would speak of him so often over the years that the stranger would become dear to me. "The world's greatest poet," Funes said in a hyperbolic claim, reiterating Pasquiano's genius as he glared at the picture from the paper.

Then, Funes went on to pay further homage to his friend Pasquiano, with us as audience. In my view, it was his way of telling me who he was, and who I would be dealing with. As the rain intensified on the flimsy metal roof, Funes took an envelope from his pocket, an unopened letter with a noble-looking red wax seal, a replica of a love letter of yore, and soberly revealed that the envelope held Domingo Pasquiano's latest poem.

"From April," he said, slitting the seal with a dirty knife and showing us a page of type-written lines. He held them in such a way that suggested they contained sacred verse.

Funes then leapt to his feet, exalted. My friend and I were left at the table, dumbstruck and motionless in our seats, as his cigarette burned away in the ashtray, the thread of smoke rising in a thin, perfect column. We watched him descend the front steps onto the lawn and come to a stop several meters from the house. Our view was framed by the open door: we could see the clothes out on the line and the two dark grooves of the lane leading to the house amid the green expanse of patchy grass and weeds left to grow knee-high, and farther out the trees and turbulent gray sky that steeped the afternoon in premature darkness. Had lightning flashed in the background, we might have been observing an El Greco painting; and yet the scene before us was actually a serene one, more apt for private confession than that sort of mystical or tragic excess. And yet we were witnessing a miracle, the miracle of Funes's surrender to the dream born in the dusty streets of Mexico City and the miracle of his unbreakable friendship with Pasquiano and the miracle of the vernal oaths he'd sworn as a young Negationist poet, vows he bore as if they had been branded with fire on his chest and to which he remained loyal, despite distance and the passing years.

"A single copy, one reading ere the flames: that's what Pasquiano's poems are for," Funes said suddenly, addressing us through the doorway, grateful that, for once, his friend's work would enjoy a small audience before falling into eternal silence. That was the purpose of the correspondence they kept up for many years, despite the Atlantic Ocean and thousands of kilometers between them: a text written for one ephemeral reading, a ceremony celebrated in a distant country in the strangeness of the afternoon, no pretense of permanence, no expectation for how the lines might resonate. What seemed to matter to Pasquiano, the only way he deemed his message heard, was knowing that somewhere, someone fervently read his words for a brief moment in time.

Funes performed his ritual and I considered what kind of madman we had met deep in the woods. He held himself with the gravitas befitting a liturgy: his sandaled feet were planted firmly in the mud, hair plastered with rain, and, through the wet shirt, his skin had taken on an amphibious quality, a hybrid texture. The dog barked as she leapt around him, and we strained to hear the beginning of Pasquiano's verses.

The poem was short, no longer than a minute or two, but it was raining hard and the paper disintegrated so rapidly that Funes barely had time to finish reading it. When the page was a crumbled mess in his hands, the only copy of the poem gone forever, he looked up at us, as if some type of consecration had taken place.

"That's it."

Funes let the pieces fall to the ground, untroubled when the dog trampled the inert page. I studied the perfect tube of ash the cigarette had become.

∞

The theatrics of our first meeting very well could have given me an inaccurate impression of Ricardo Funes. But although he was fond of controversy, there was genuinely nothing artificial about him. He wasn't one to chase recognition for his literary merit through such extravagances, unlike the many other aspiring poets I had met by that stage who—despite a lack of both talent and a minimal foundation in literary studies—performed their circus antics in the Raval, rending their T-shirts or dumping buckets of red paint over their heads, desperate in their attempts to draw an audience.

In contrast, Funes never came up with ways to flaunt his uniqueness; instead, he constructed a fictional universe all his own, with its particular symbology and myths. There was a basis for his peculiarity: he lived an isolated life, obsessed with literature and a past he tended to idealize, forever unsuccessful in his bids to establish a connection with others who shared his angst. He was marooned on an island without peers to serve as mirrors and reflect his potential feats or failures.

After the day I watched him read Pasquiano's fleeting verses in the rain, it was a long time before I saw Funes again. In fact, five years passed before our paths crossed, this time in Barcelona, at the launch of my latest novel at what was then the most popular bookstore in the city. Given that I hadn't extended him an invitation, I took it that Funes had turned up on his own accord to substantiate our friendship, which had been deferred as soon as it began.

I noticed him only after I had finished speaking, when I looked up and recognized him at the back of the store. He stood apart from the little cliques that had formed, leaning against a shelf stacked with books. At the time, he would have been thirty-five and I forty, though with Funes age was a paradoxical phenomenon: sometimes he seemed like a teenager, with his playfulness and bursts of enthusiasm and ability to keep his oldest fantasies intact, and other times he gave the impression of being much older, perhaps because he had peered into more abysses in fewer years than most. And though he didn't have his farmer sandals or noisy dog, he presented just as odd an image, conspicuous in his round, Victorian clerk's glasses, bony jaw, and scrawny mien. He wore a long gabardine coat, a style that might have suggested capitulation to the tritest of literary stereotypes: the austere writer, the self-serious novelist— one of those sad sorts who delights in his own failure—or worse still, the melancholy Parisian poet; in Funes's case, however, it was simply that he had gotten it on sale for next to nothing.

I started toward him, and before we'd even had a chance to say hello, I watched him demonstrate the same spirited disposition he'd shown years before when, as he stepped past a critic who had written several articles about my work, Funes got in one of his unexpected barbs: "I have tried, you know. But it's impossible: you talk about literature and it's like reading an appliance manual—half the words are incomprehensible." Before the man could react, Funes reached out and shook my hand warmly, not at all bitter about the years-long stretch of silence between us.

I quickly learned the reason for the long hiatus in our communication: he had been writing to me at the wrong address, I didn't know in which remote, provincial village he had landed as a traveling peddler, and our mutual professor friend had also lost track of Funes's trail.

Whatever the reasons, that was how Ricardo Funes and I found each other again, and how I discovered that he was living in Lloret de Mar, where he had been drawn to settle after so much drifting around. He promptly invited me to visit him in the coastal town, promising me that—as far as he was concerned—nothing essential had changed: "The same coffee and cigarettes, Fernando," he said.

I accepted, of course, in part because I was intrigued by Funes's near visceral dedication to literature, despite having never reaped any reward whatsoever for his concerted efforts, and in part because I felt obliged given my bad manners of having let five years go by without a single word.

And so, years after visiting on some long-ago family vacation, I returned to Lloret. I took the train from Barcelona, a trip I would repeat on innumerable occasions over the course of the next fifteen years. He asked me to meet him in a café in the center of town, La Fundamental, an establishment with no aspiration other than to supply office workers with their morning coffee and serve tea and pastries to elderly ladies in the afternoon. I quickly surmised that the café also served as Funes's usual stomping ground.

For the first few minutes, we retraced the terrain of our conversation in his cabin on the outskirts of Castelldefels, but he also confessed that he rarely wrote poetry anymore, concentrating his efforts on the genres of short fiction and novel instead. And smiling broadly, he revealed that he had gotten married and was unimaginably happy: "She tends the garden and I try to beat the house," he said, underscoring the gratitude he felt for his wife's confidence in him. She worked at the Lloret de Mar town hall, while he dedicated himself exclusively to chasing sporadic income with his stories.

He was, he said, a very satisfied man. And yet, he had already begun to be afflicted by the pain that would pursue him until his death: the awareness of growing old, that our days are numbered and seem to accelerate with the passage of time. I was surprised by the prophetic nature of his musings, which seem to represent a kind of regret foretold.

A cigarette dangled from his lips as he spoke, the ember slowly consumed, the ash falling under the burden of its own weight: "Every written page is a gamble—hit the jackpot or lose the bet." The cigarette burned and the smoke rose toward the ceiling as Funes pondered the number of hours he had spent in the libraries of Mexico City, marveling at the ease with which he used to memorize whole pages by the authors who most excited him, and deriding the other drivel on which he had squandered precious hours of his youth.

Rough-shaven, his curls cropped shorter than when I first met him, Funes moved and expressed himself with natural elegance, the result of an unshakeable confidence in who he was and what he was capable of. He gave an account of his exorbitant reading habits, sighing in conclusion: "I am an uneducated and very well-read man."

Funes had received me with a file folder and folded newspaper at his usual table by the wall. Over the course of the two hours we were there, I noted that the waiter brought him coffee without being asked. When Funes went to pay, he handed the man a paper napkin with a few scribbled lines instead of reaching for his wallet. This unusual form of payment was a running joke between them.

"Hey, it's like we've told you: we might serve the coffee but we're nobody's patron," replied the veteran waiter from behind the counter. He was over sixty, at least, and struck me as vaguely paternal. "How about a few coins instead?"

Funes laughed, protesting that the obligation to pay with actual money constituted an insult, given that he was accompanied by a man as illustrious as myself. He gave the man a wink as he settled the bill and left the small change for a tip. "Suit yourself," he said. "But you might've just passed on a Picasso."

Funes paid his respects to the cook—the waiter's wife, apparently—and we left, chatting as we strolled the streets of Lloret, which I had never visited in autumn. Funes carried his folder and the newspaper tucked under his arm. It was October, a month in which the sun shone low and the imminent cold threatened, a month that augured the tourists' retreat and the approaching emptiness of winter, but which still retained a memory of bustling terraces and bodies in bathing suits. A cursory look sufficed to see that the majority of units in the newer apartment buildings were already closed up and some of the local shops shuttered for the season. Nevertheless, the beach's beauty and the vestiges of the original seaside village made it a pleasant place to live.

In autumn, Lloret was undoubtedly an appropriate place for locals to recoup the peace stolen from them during the high season, or for English retirees who sought the tenuous Mediterranean sunlight as respite from the eternal fog of Britain, but it seemed to me a place ill-suited for a Peruvian poet who, in his youth, had aspired to revolutionize Mexican poetry, and who still believed he would one day write something to vindicate the seemingly-doomed venture he had pursued his whole life.

Funes interrupted my reflections with the invitation to join him on his daily rounds, a desultory routine that bore resemblance to that of an unemployed bureaucrat. Though I hadn't given him any indication of when I planned to catch the return train to Barcelona, he guided me down to the deserted beach. I observed him as we strolled: Funes would step firmly for a minute or two, then turn back to regard his tracks in the sand, and if seagulls came close, stamp to stir them into flight. Witnessing him in his natural habitat, I thought about just how much free time the man had, and how little stimulation other than the arrival of Domingo Pasquiano's poems at the beginning of each month.

Every now and again, he paused briefly before the quiet sea, which was as cold as an inland lake, its glitter dulled by the flat October light, and regaled me with tales of Dutch tourists drowned in the treacherous tides of the Costa Brava, or revealed the favorite coves of local nudists—his preferred way to swim, incidentally—before setting off again. He only stopped for good upon reaching the far end of the beach, where a rock formation rose like a maritime monument. "My favorite spot, obviously," he joked, acknowledging his Romantic spirit as he studied the rocks anchored in the sand.

It hadn't escaped my notice that Funes held the folder close to his body for the duration of our walk, as if it contained valuable documents. I was sure it contained a novel he planned to ask me to show a publisher, but I soon discovered that wasn't the case.

We turned to make our way back to the train station. On the way, Funes ducked into the post office, where he behaved with the same degree of familiarity as in the café. He greeted the security guard with a brief exchange about the results of a match between their rival soccer teams, as if it were a daily greeting of the lobby concierge upon arriving at the office.

He strode to the clerk's window and handed over the four envelopes tucked in the folder. "We're traveling to all corners of the peninsula today: Ourense, Huesca, Seville, and Murcia."

Funes was submitting his stories to literary contests, the kind sponsored by towns and small cities across the whole of Spain, the lottery he played in hopes of making a small contribution to the family income. I confess, I felt pity at the sight of the brown envelopes addressed in marker; the starkness of the contrast between such meager hope and the glitter with which he recounted his adolescence in Mexico.

Funes tossed a coin in the air, catching and concealing it between his palms, as the post office clerk weighed the envelopes and applied the corresponding labels, then pronounced his ruling.

"Tails."

He was correct. He handed Funes his change and a receipt.

"There you go: a nice check and another plaque in the living room by Christmas."

The assertion, delivered in the spirit of optimism, was absolutely terrible.

For a man like Funes, a man who had devoted so much time, so much effort to his writing, a man who had lived like a lay monk, a supplicant to his stories, to accept a statement like the clerk's was to reveal the extent to which he had acquiesced to his situation on the tightrope of perpetual uncertainty, resigned to the belief that neither his talent nor will were enough: subject to the winds of chance, the very same book might be cast into the fire, or whisked away toward the most prestigious spotlight.

In the end, the coin toss represented Funes's acceptance that although he could very well devote his whole life to writing the most marvelous of books, ultimately it was possible the only recognition he would ever receive would be legendary tales of his misfortune or a few hagiographic write-ups in honor of his centenary. Countless writers before him had suffered a similar fate, and Funes was surely aware that a great many excellent books are only freed from the oblivion of the desk drawer long after their authors have been consumed by worms.

☙

The truth was that Funes's early, unhappy situation was not entirely unwarranted, nor was it simply the case of an author being discovered late in life: I myself read his manuscripts for years, and found them to be erratic texts, lacking their own cohesive themes and tone, fragments in which one could barely glean the greatness of his poetics to come. And then—in a shot of desperation—he wrote *The Aztec*, a novel whose unexpected authorial maturity would come to suffuse all of his subsequent works. The faltering voice of his earlier attempts took on resounding authority at last, and his characters, heretofore rough sketches, assumed their majestic forms. It was a novel in which Funes consummated his long-gestated revenge: the revindication of his life and countryless past. When read with care, the text offered a portrait of Funes himself, a portrait in which he exaggerated his nomadism and the instability of his huckster's life and the many adventures he weathered, clutching his poet's notebooks. The novel barely made reference to the nearly two solitary decades he spent writing on his computer, isolated in Lloret: instead, it was a hero's story, brimming with light and enthusiasm, a myth supported by his enviable biography.

The book's unbridled success came as a surprise to all, even to me. As time marched on, I had begun to lose faith in him, though I continued to visit Lloret, armed with no excuse except my fondness for him and his intelligent reflections. Truth be told, I was skeptical of the phenomenon that was to come, and rather amazed that Funes stayed put on his lonely poet's promontory for so long, an aging adolescent, dogged before the waves, regardless of the fact that his future rested on his chances in those municipal story contests, whose juries were comprised of local cultural councilmen and high school teachers.

છ

Funes often met me at the train station—if he had a productive morning—or at his usual table in La Fundamental, and we filled the hours with endless conversation about the many subjects he was capable of arguing over until the sun went down. It took me several years to finally understand that the miracle of our adult friendship, in which neither party sought to benefit from the other, was owed to Funes's innate character: Ricardo Funes didn't conceive of relationships in terms other than complete acceptance or total rejection, to the extent that he either ignored you forever—regardless of your efforts—or you fell prey to a net from which you would never manage to escape.

Over time, I came to take part in his usual habits during my visits to his seaside retreat. Some mornings, I accompanied him to the town hall where his wife, Guadalupe, worked, and although he often made the excuse that we ought to take advantage of the office air-conditioning or decent heaters, I noticed that he always brought flowers or a box of chocolates, or news of an award, as if he were aware of the need to honor the generosity of his patroness. Funes never forgot Guadalupe's sacrifice, typing letters eight hours a day so that he could devote himself to his stories undisturbed, so confident in his work that when Funes lost heart, his wife was the one to reassure him of his talent.

Life in Lloret had its drawbacks. The town offered few attractions apart from visiting the café where he'd earned the distinction of his own table, a perk usually granted only to retirees, or walking his envelopes over to the post office, or frequenting the hobby store—he was obsessed with battle reenactments—or the periodic drama of becoming embroiled in political arguments with the owner of the neighborhood newsstand and other pencil-pushers at his wife's office, or scuffling with gangs of Russian tourists who, for weeks on end in the summer, woke him up with their noisy cars. And then there was the scourge of winter, when the columns of empty tourist apartments gave Lloret the air of a dismal stage set of a town abandoned post-plague.

We didn't always see each other in his seaside kingdom. On occasion, Funes came to his old city of Barcelona to peruse discount bookshops or appear at my home, unannounced. Often, he simply turned up at my events, a ubiquitous phantom. He so grew to enjoy the challenge of materializing without warning that he developed the peculiar custom of greeting me with a finger pressed against my back as if it were a pistol, and a sentence that betrayed his familiarity with violence—apparently acquired in his impetuous youth—as well as a premonition of his disease.

"And thus Death arrives: without an appointment."

Our conversations in the cafés of the Raval—where Funes claimed to have written several books—or on the seaside promenade in the Barceloneta—before the neighborhood became infested with tourists—were where Funes was most inspired to reconstruct his youth, a youth he described as if it were a legend, someone else's legend, an epic poem protagonized by another man, yet his to recite, as if all of Funes's important memories could be ascribed to that narrow window of time.

Through his tales, I managed to glean a rough sketch of his life: from the time he touched down in Barcelona with his mother, who had separated from his father by then, through his years moonlighting at odd jobs, and eventually to his position as family man in Lloret.

But the time he spoke of most often, the time he had been happiest and still pined for, was his spell in Mexico City and his participation in the feats of the *negacionismo* movement. To hear him tell it, the movement was of such importance to Mexico's poetic geography that if news of it hadn't reached Europe, it was only because of the irrelevance of the lyrical genre. In a drama that recalled the myths of the New York mafia, Funes claimed that he and Pasquiano came to control a Mexico City contraband-tobacco trafficking network so important that, in addition to the haze of cash-bloated wallets and product stashed in car trunks, they had to contend with the risk of being caught in the crossfire between rival gangs. But the worst damage inflicted by that business was to his health: he was a tobacco addict, of the sort that squirreled away packs of cigarettes in the fridge or inside his mattress, and he was always finding threads of loose tobacco on the silverware or his pillow. The sheer quantity of cigarettes, lit or not, had meant the total contamination of his lungs. "But I've actually been spitting up blood for a long time," he clarified once, explaining the reasons for his characteristic cough and maintaining that his ailment was entirely natural and unrelated to his cigarette consumption.

If our meetings in Barcelona were an excuse for Funes to detail some of the highlights from his life in Mexico City and in Peru, they were also a way for me to learn which apartment building he had lived in, on which street, or which bar still had the same name as when he discovered it, or which books he wrote each year he lived in the city, and what he titled them. This was how I became aware of another of his most notable interests: a predilection for erotic films, pornography, really, on which he offered technical commentary akin to that of an opera lover, attending screenings in the specialized theaters of Barcelona with his friend Rodolfo García Huertas, another aspiring novelist I had never heard of, who had been featured in a few barely relevant anthologies and with whom Funes had drawn up plans for a small artisanal press years earlier. The internet didn't exist in those days and all cities had erotic movie theaters on their secluded downtown streets. After the showing, there was little room for my third-party interjections in the discussion between the two old friends who had traipsed the streets of Barcelona together. "Her pussy is a mess," I heard Funes assert once upon leaving the theater, while García Huertas—whom I came to recognize as Funes's closest companion in Spain, since the early days—compared the actress's enthusiasm or ennui to her comportment in other films. It was the first time I had heard pornography discussed without the pulse of arousal, discussed simply for aesthetic pleasure and the merits of an art form in its own right. I didn't dare say a word until they tired of their cinematographic analysis.

García Huertas's arrival on the scene also meant I had someone with whom I could share my concerns with respect to my new friend. Once, while Funes lagged behind to argue with the ticket seller at one of the theaters, García Huertas and I waited in a café on Plaça Catalunya. As I observed the lights from passing traffic through the window, I took the opportunity to express my doubts over some of our mutual friend's claims: Funes had told me that in the fight for control over the underground tobacco market, he had come to sleep with a knife under his pillow at all times, for example; or that one night, he fled his own house through the sewer in order to avoid reprisal.

I was, I suppose, generally questioning his past and the credibility of his word.

"He lies," I said, looking García Huertas in the eye.

García Huertas had met Funes every day for years and shared more tea and coffee and bookstore visits with him than anyone in Barcelona. So deeply rooted was their affinity and confidence in one another that they had established a reciprocal pact in which one would transcribe the other's words so that nothing but pure storytelling was required of the person who was submerged in the midst of the creative process. He did not share my misgivings.

"Don't try to figure out what deserves an encyclopedia entry and what doesn't," he said, revealing that Funes had told him the same anecdote two different ways, one in which he was the victim and another as the aggressor. "He talks about what he writes as if it had really happened, and he writes what actually happened as if it were made up: he stirs it all together until there's not an uncontaminated ingredient in the pot."

&

Between his visits to Barcelona and my escapes from the tumult of the big city, my dealings with Ricardo Funes became so frequent that despite the differences in our life circumstances, I came to be treated as another fixture in his family. If I stayed in Lloret later than planned, if night fell and I missed the last train back to the city, I would have dinner with him and Guadalupe in their little two-room house that was like a student apartment, and invariably sleep on the sofa in the room that served as library and living room, chock full of books and magazines and various boxes stuffed with stacks of unpublished manuscripts.

As one could imagine, Funes's idiosyncrasies were reflected in his home, which was an old apartment in a low dwelling in the historic district, boxed between streets so narrow that they blocked views of the sea, and the thick walls retained so much dampness that in the winter they were forced to resort to electric heaters and wearing gloves and scarves indoors. Still, the wide front windows let in beautiful light. I recall perfectly the first time I entered the living room and had the sensation of going back in time to a child's playroom. Model airplanes hung by string suspended from the ceiling, there were little leaden figures from Napoleon's armies, each military dress coat and flag hand-painted by Funes himself, and plants cluttered every corner and table and bookshelf in a concession to Guadalupe, who came from a green mountain village in the north of Girona and yearned to live surrounded by flora, even in their coastal locale.

I enjoyed the privileges of a long-absent guest on those evenings. They insisted I sit in the living room at the table draped in a red and white checkered tablecloth and dotted with breadcrumbs or bits of food, and refused to let me help with anything. My only duty was to converse with them as each performed his or her assigned domestic responsibility: Guadalupe was in charge of cooking and Funes responsible for washing dishes and cutlery, or performing the coarser tasks of peeling potatoes and beating eggs. I took this homey tableau as proof of their years of conjugal bliss: as they stood at the counter camouflaged by plants with tendrils cascading like jungle vines, their backs to me, Funes hid the knife or the salt shaker Guadalupe needed, or cried exaggerated tears as he chopped onions. "Remember these years of poverty," he would joke, drawing near so she could dry the tears on his cheeks, "when we finally live in a mansion."

That was how Funes had seduced her. He'd had no money and no certain future, but was gifted with enthusiasm and a convincing confidence that an exceptional life awaited.

It was that very same fantastical nature that ensured a good number of those evenings revolved around his ideas.

Some nights, he cajoled us into watching a porn film, pausing during the most explicit scenes and pointing out the director's aesthetic, while Guadalupe and I laughed at his critiques of that peculiar art form. On other occasions, he spun stories for the pure pleasure of hearing himself talk, like when he claimed Pasquiano was orphaned of both mother and father, with no family except a sister on her deathbed with a degenerative disease, only to confess an hour—and a multitude of heartrending laments—later that he had made it all up and there was nothing at all to feel bad about.

"I don't get you two," he said when Guadalupe and I protested that the joke was in poor taste. "It's like you'd prefer his pain to be real."

But it wasn't always fun and games and happy performances.

On the contrary, his failure to publish was often an obstacle to his affability. If he put a lot of hope into a story for some contest or other and didn't win, or if he compared his age with the authors who were already publishing with prestigious houses, or others who preceded us both, writers we admired and whose bibliography we knew down to the last detail, he had to admit he would never bask in the beauty of early success, and even doubted his future prospects for triumph. "I'll have an anonymous grave: just another dead guy," he said on an especially pessimistic day, when he revealed his hunch that he was destined to die before publishing a single book. And if months passed without a single prize check in the mailbox, like a hunter who spent his ammunition but returns home without game, he flippantly mocked his own failure by subjecting himself to various forms of self-flagellation: a crown of thorns, for example, set atop his head like a martyred pagan, or choosing to stand in the corner for the duration of dinner, a stack of books in each hand like a naughty schoolboy.

There were bleaker moments, too, when he lost the will to indulge his sense of humor. With undisguised misgivings about his future, he wrote furious letters to the editors who rejected his submissions, or to literary critics if they favored one of their friends, or even to novelists of his generation who didn't adequately appreciate his attempts to establish contact. I knew he spent afternoons at La Fundamental submerged in prolonged silence, immobile before the window, watching the pleasure boats bobbing on the tide in anticipation of summer, or the outdoor cafés on the promenade, their chairs and tables chained up for the season, the very reflection of Funes himself, who had been plunged into a lull, an unbearable armistice, capitulation following years of effort for naught.

His disgruntled and impotent displays became more frequent over time, revealing desperation over his failure to achieve what he had hoped, taking a darker turn and culminating in a night when Funes would most eloquently express his despair and I would finally understand just how much it hurt him to have never received even minimal acknowledgement for his work. We were at their little house, having dinner, and Funes was doing his crown-of-thorns bit, the crown that was really a kind of halo he had fashioned out of dry twigs. To dramatize his penitence, he set a large altar candle in the center of his plate and stated that he was taking a vow of silence until the time when he could produce something of sufficient merit to redeem himself. "If my words can't convince a prize jury, I don't deserve to open my mouth," he'd said.

"Oh, why don't you walk on broken glass while you're at it," Guadalupe said. She set a metal pot full of pasta on the table. "For our guest's sake, you could at least speak. You've been playing this game all day and you're going to faint."

She grabbed a fork and shoved it, pasta-laden, toward his mouth.

"Eat."

She continued to insist, as if attempting to feed a stubborn child, a sulky child who refused to be touched, a disconsolate child on the verge of tears. Funes pressed his lips together tightly and turned his head.

I had the sense of witnessing something I shouldn't, alien to the intimacy of the moment. A bead of sweat dripped from Funes's brow. His martyrdom was of sweat, not blood, since his crown had no thorns to prick his skin and since he wore a thick sweater in the June heat, an ingenious attempt to intensify his self-inflicted torment. He refused the food and she refused to surrender. In the silence, I heard a heavy droplet drip from the faucet.

Funes looked at me in a way he never had before, more expressive than during any previous confession: his eyes were damp, wounded by a dormant pain he wouldn't dare name, a kind of imprisonment he fought in secret. We didn't know then that he suffered from writer's block, an aphonia of the page, so intense that he was about to lose his mind.

Guadalupe and I finished the meal in a somber mood, Funes like a mannequin at the table, obdurate in his insistence that he had been misunderstood his whole life. I bid him goodnight, and Guadalupe walked me to the door.

"You are very important to him," she said, as we heard the sound of Funes rifling through folders and books in his office, still cloistered in his silence.

It wasn't until hours later, the next day, in Barcelona, that I was struck by just how much, in his anguish, Funes had resembled a doomsday prophet, or demented scientist: there among the WWII bombers and miniature Napoleonic mercenaries, walls replete with books and the foliage of Guadalupe's plants, it was as if he had decided to assemble his own world, a universe suitable for him alone, because he could no longer abide the one outside his door.

☙

Eventually, Funes ventured from his usual haunts—La Fundamental and his own living room—and rented a space in which to write—a cellar across the street from their apartment, a kind storage space that went from housing old furniture to serving as a studio for his computer and stacks of paper.

As time passed, the long cycle of submission, waiting,

rejection, the economic belt-tightening, and daily assaults of innumerable anxieties were all heightened, especially after the birth of his son Patricio, a factor that forced Funes to combine his work as a writer—engrossed in sagas no one would read—with a governess's duties. His son became like another limb, and as the child grew, one of Funes's most important missions seemed to be inculcating Patricio with his own particular view of reality, including relationships: "See this gentleman here?" he once said to a three-year-old Patricio, pointing at me as we hiked to the lookout at the Castell d'en Plaja, the turreted storybook castle with the best views of Lloret. "He's the captain of our army." Later, we sat dangling our feet over the cliff's edge, interrupting our adult conversation to tell the boy old sailor stories and inspire him with the time-honored appreciation for a pirate's freedom.

In actuality, fatherhood didn't change Funes, unless it was to intensify his determination to succeed as a writer, despite the fact that a less hopeful future hardly seemed possible. By then, more often than not, Funes could be found immersed inside fantasies and dulcet depictions of his youth. He still clung to the remnants of a mythologized adolescence, kept alive by bursts of oxygen he got from reliving memories of his adventures when he was just seventeen or eighteen years old. It was as if he was compelled to repeat those rhetorical exercises, looping accounts that rehashed the same stories—difficult for his listener to share in, incidentally—all in order to justify his ambition to live an epic life. Funes's sleepy existence in Lloret had condemned him to too protracted a ceasefire, even for a patient warrior like himself.

While he amassed rejection letters from a host of publishing houses, Funes maintained written correspondence with one man: Domingo Pasquiano. For me, Pasquiano had always represented a ghostly interlocutor, but García Huertas had actually met him during a brief visit Pasquiano made to Barcelona while Funes lived there, a visit which served to confirm Funes's inflexibility in his demands that others adhere to his principles of loyalty. According to García Huertas, Pasquiano had come all the way to Barcelona with the sole purpose of aiding Funes in a plot to settle a score with another poet, who also had arrived from Mexico in search of his own European adventure. In an unforgivable abuse of Funes's hospitality, the young man—they were all young men, then—took advantage of the long hours Funes worked with his mother to weasel his way into the good graces of the Catalan student who was Funes's girlfriend at the time. "They would have chucked him into a pool wearing cement shoes," García Huertas concluded, amused by the memory of Funes and Pasquiano handcuffing the traitor to a lamppost on a busy street, naked and gagged and exposed to the curious neighbors, until he was freed by officers of the Catalonian police force, the *Mossos d'Esquadra*.

The affair was a classic example of the strict codes of nobility by which the *negacionistas* lived. But as the years passed, Funes was to experience the particular ache reserved for a person with such distinct hatreds and

35

passions: the blow of witnessing how the old members of his Negationist sect forgot their youthful vows. For Funes, no passage of time could justify those desertions. Every time some old associate flouted the tenets of that strange society, every time one of its participants praised a powerful poet, spurned the group by ceasing to collaborate in some underground journal, or committed some other form of betrayal, Pasquiano would send a succinct letter informing him of the treachery, at which point Funes would proceed to exorcize the offender's legacy from European shores, ripping pages out of an anthology in which they'd both appeared, scribbling out the traitor's face in a group picture, or prohibiting the mention of his name, all in ceremonies akin to a private funeral—exact copies of the rituals his friend Pasquiano performed on the other side of the Atlantic.

There was no worse vengeance against those renegade poets than the elimination of every line they had written, right down to the very last syllable. There were times when he threw whole volumes off a cliff, when he fashioned the pages into paper boats and shipped them out to sea, watching them sink as if they were galleons, or fed them to his dog in little wadded up balls, proffering the same insults he would have liked to deliver to their faces: "You look like an altar boy, you kiss-ass rat-soul," he cursed the sellout of the moment, photographed shaking the hand of a noted public figure in a news clipping sent by Pasquiano.

Funes would have defended his poetic comrades like a brother, had the need arisen, and I was well aware of the sting brought by the news of each fresh heresy. But one afternoon in January or February, I witnessed the extent to which the defections wounded him. He had received some of the worst news imaginable: the abdication of one of the movement's three founding members, a man who, in addition to joining in the literary guerilla movement alongside Funes and Pasquiano, had assumed the role of comptroller in their contraband tobacco business. Now all of a sudden, the former *negacionista* wanted any evidence of his involvement erased so that he could enjoy a cushy bureaucratic position at the embassy in Paris.

I have never seen Funes so furious. It was five or six o'clock in the evening, a time of day with little light in the winter months. The cold had set in and a lugubrious atmosphere reigned, a presage of the coming night and drawing of the curtains. On the vast, empty beach, the sense of having been forsaken couldn't have been greater. We were down by the water's edge, at the far end beside the rock formation Funes favored. He stood with his hands jammed in his pockets. The sea breeze ruffled his hair, and for the first time I had the sudden suspicion that perhaps his signature round glasses served not only to correct the nearsightedness he'd known since childhood, but as a shield to camouflage his disappointment. There was a strange look in his eye, as if he strained to discern some distant, irrecoverable place, as if—just beyond the dusky horizon—he could make out the Mexican coast, a paradise of bygone youth and his first stop in exile, despite the fact Mexico did not lie across the Mediterranean, but in precisely the opposite direction.

As he chewed on his grievances, he didn't look at me once, or notice his dog barking and running to and fro, or shoo away the gulls pecking at the stray seaweed and other flotsam dragged in by the tide. He was focused purely on the task of spilling his hate into the refuge of the sea. I stood with him in silence, riveted by the froth and foam begotten by the waves as they crashed onto the rocks. We were alone on the stretch of sand, save for a man I spied walking toward us slowly from the other end of the beach, just along the sea's edge, his head bowed to observe the sand below his bare feet, shoes in hand and pant legs rolled up.

At some point, Funes was unable to contain his rage and in a sudden, violent move, he hurled Pasquiano's letter and the newspaper tucked under his arm into the sea as far as he could.

It was a short flight. The papers landed a dozen meters offshore, not far enough to liberate him from the crush of disillusion.

"That's it! Sink! Sink! Be gone forever."

Funes's dog barked at the tide, agitated by the repetitive cadence of the waves and the sigh of the sea at dusk, as the letter and scattered newspaper pages washed repeatedly over the rocks. The other man, the beachcomber, picked up his pace and walked away from us, startled by Funes's abrupt gesture. I imagined fancifully that we looked like dangerous men to him, co-conspirators plotting some kind of revenge. Overhead, a flock of gulls circled the rocks, mistaking the papers my friend had flung for the cadavers of several small rodents.

I was compelled to ask the question that had dogged me for some time.

"How many of you are there left?"

Funes turned to me. His glasses were splattered with sea spray, and I wondered how the waves had managed to graze him. And seeing him so thin, so deserted on that absurd shore where he had run aground long before, so removed from his youth and blazing days as a subversive poet and kingpin in the clandestine cigarette market in Mexico City, I stood in solidarity against his impotence and the consciousness that he waged an ever more solitary battle on foreign soil.

"Two," he said, a revelation that contained as much shame as conviction, as much sorrow for the poet companions he lost along the way as determination to stay the course on his own. "Each on his own continent."

FERNANDO VALLÉS I AM NOT. I haven't published any novels or poetry collections or written for a newspaper, but I can also talk about Ricardo Funes, like Fernando has decided to do.

My name is Guadalupe, Guadalupe Mora. That's *my* real name, but I don't mind calling the man who was my husband Ricardo Funes.

His name isn't really important. It's his story that matters most: it matters that for twenty years he lived the life of a premature retiree in Lloret de Mar, a civil servant without a post, a soldier waiting for the order to mobilize to the front line of a battle that never did come. It matters that he accumulated so many dreams and desires in his desk drawer that he was like a dam ready to burst because no cement wall is strong enough to resist such pressure.

All the while, I slept next to him. I watched him write at the kitchen table and in his basement study and in cafés, awake all night, convinced there were paragraphs in his mind that would vanish if he went to bed. I watched him read while standing in the street, oblivious to whether the light had turned green, mesmerized by the discovery of some unknown writer. I watched him turn desperate as the years passed and the rejection letters piled up and he got no recognition except for an occasional first prize in a town writing contest.

No matter how many times publishers ignored the manuscripts he sent, he was so stubborn and had so much faith in his own talent that he was determined to keep trying, even as he had to accept the risk that he would die without ever having published a single book. Taking into account his trajectory as a whole, I contend that he should be commended for the days he toiled without hope of compensation, rather than the time when whatever he did received unanimous approval.

For my part, I came to know his obsessive personality and unflagging tenacity early on, when he tried to seduce me. The truth is, I didn't resist him nearly as hard as editors resisted his work.

I met him in Besalú, the village in Girona where I was born, and where Ricardo arrived with his mother, who decided to set up a notions shop there. That spring, I was twenty years old and had abandoned the university, disappointed with the classes. I didn't know what I wanted to do or how I wanted to live. I wasn't working, except to help out around my house, and I was looking for a job that would allow me to move out.

When they blew into the village, Ricardo and his mother looked like escapees from the caravan of carnies and jewelry sellers who came for the local fair every year, quintessential small-time peddlers who spent their summers traveling from town to town. In their case, this usually seasonal activity was apparently permanent. They were well-versed in the common techniques of their trade. His mother rented a storefront near the castle, the area most popular with tourists, while Ricardo laid out his assortment of belts and wallets and hats at a different strategic point: the esplanade under the shadow of the Roman arches that spanned the river Fluvià, a few meters from the medieval bridge at the entrance to town. The ideal spot to convince visitors of the unbeatable prices and exceptional quality of his goods, all with the aid of his trusty megaphone.

As I passed his stall one morning, glancing at the rickety setup—a skeletal metal contraption and a piece of canvas that provided a little rectangle of shade—Ricardo besieged me with the same obnoxious ploy he used on tourists to sell his belts, calling to me through his megaphone and, when he saw that I didn't slow down or respond, following after me. Apparently unconcerned about the possibility that someone might steal his merchandise, he walked the whole span of the bridge, calling out the same amplified refrain through the megaphone. He bid me farewell at the other side of the bridge, promising: "I won't stop until you agree to dinner." He spoke as if addressing a large crowd at a protest, with a mix of humor and resolve that made me feel he would make good on his word.

The gambit was repeated over the following weeks. My initial reaction was to reject him, of course: the huckster routine was so embarrassing. I could have dodged him if I'd wanted to. I could have avoided his barbican at the village gates and found other, more direct points of entry. But the truth is, his pursuit had quickly become an exhilarating game for us both. Every time I passed the little wooden stall from which he had chosen to lay siege to the village—at least until he ran out of things to sell—Ricardo would stop haggling with tourists and amble after me, megaphone in hand, as if he were my escort with a duty to pay me compliments while I made my journey across the bridge. Ricardo displayed an inexhaustible verbosity from the very beginning, gushing over the various characters he assigned to me: the washerwoman carrying water in an earthenware pitcher, the princess imprisoned in her tower, the young wife condemned to marry an already-old man. He tried to make me laugh, to seduce me with his antics, and I encouraged him—despite the scandal our little parade caused. We reprised our performance until I finally accepted his proposal from the first day: "Dinner. Tomorrow," I said. I had already decided weeks before that I wanted to get to know him, once I'd watched him invent all sorts of stories to sell his bags and seen him writing and reading at a folding table he put out next to his van. I wanted to know him, despite the fact that, back then, his being Peruvian was an exoticism that demanded a certain amount of wariness, and in my house they talked about "the foreigner" as if he were a vagabond bum.

Ricardo was ten years older than me, and I had never met anyone like him. In my world, everything he did was unparalleled. I found him so wonderfully odd, he enjoyed himself in the funniest ways—he wanted us to swim naked in the river at night, or watch the stars lying on our backs on one of Besalú's dolmens, he was fond of throwing pebbles at my window instead of calling me on the phone, he left me notes under the doormat—but mostly, Ricardo was exceptional because he lived his life as if his sole objective was to relish everything he did, in order to remember it later. He conserved that trait, unconsciously, perhaps, his entire life. He loved telling stories so much that he seemed to put a greater or lesser value on every experience according to the shine it would add to his biography. Partly because of his anecdotist's nature and partly because he tended to exalt his memories, I could never quite tell which exploits had actually happened and which ones he'd made up. Ricardo romanticized even the smallest feats, burnishing them until they shone with a heroic gleam.

Ricardo and I mostly saw each other outdoors, which made the most sense considering his business. We used to meet in the evening, when the tourists had abandoned Besalú. If it was hot, we went down to the river to swim, or we'd shack up in his van, where the pieces of cloth tacked up over the windows gave us more privacy. Sometimes we sat out in beach chairs at his plastic table and Ricardo would recite some of the poets he knew by heart, or we'd hike up to the pasture that overlooked the embankment where he parked his van, where millennia-old stone dolmens—another tourist draw for the town—stood amid a herd of grazing cows.

We visited the meadow at unusual hours, too, so we wouldn't have to worry about the cowherd or curious visitors nosing around the funerary stones. Ricardo would pretend to bullfight the placid cows, taking off his shirt and waving it in front of them, or would read to me by lantern, the poetry accentuated by the dense darkness, imbued with intimacy in the flickering light. The future didn't figure into our days. Maybe it was our youth, or the joy of summer, but every dream we imagined seemed possible. Tired of Barcelona's city streets and the enormity of Mexico City, Ricardo proclaimed he wanted nothing more than what he already had, that the smell of manure and the view of the medieval bridge were enough for him to write his greatest works. I brought up the possibility of reincarnation, and he was adamant: "I would do it all again. As one of these cows, even," he said, swearing he had no desire for anything to change.

And so the summer passed. We could have gone on for months more like that, if it hadn't been for an episode that forced Ricardo to leave Besalú earlier than expected, a conflict posing the risk for police questioning and legal action and which marked the first time Ricardo set the course for his departure, instead of his mother.

The fault lay with a temp job he had taken at a restaurant—the nicest one in town, on the other side of the bridge and just meters from his stall. The restaurateur entrusted him with parking the diners' cars in exchange for good money. "A month's work for two months of freedom," he told me when he took the gig. He expected he would be able to pad his earnings with tips, as well as sell his bags outside the restaurant.

Unfortunately, the potential profits threatened to have serious repercussions on his mood. The initial agreements he had made to valet soon grew to include—with no corresponding pay increase—hauling out the trash and washing the owner's Mercedes, an imposition that infuriated him. One afternoon, I found him soaping the luxury car with a sponge, rags and buckets of water littered around him. "We put up with tyrants like him in Peru," he said, forced to stay late and finish the job instead of reading in the meadow with the cows.

Between balancing his duties as valet and doorman at the restaurant and looking after his stall, Ricardo had little time to spare for reading and writing and being with me. Suddenly, the extra income and promise of more tranquil months ahead didn't compensate for the shackles imposed on him by the second job. In addition to the constraints on his time, he was obstructed by disputes over scratches and the position of the rearview mirror, as well as his irritation when forced to lug the trash into the village if the dumpster behind the restaurant filled up.

I had been on my way that evening to the esplanade where he camped in his van. Ricardo was taking me up to the pasture so he could read me some of his poems. As I approached the vehicles, I noticed right away that the headlights on his van and the boss's Mercedes were on. Visible above, the silhouettes of the cows and the dolmen's arch, and behind me the running river, the neat village houses, the cloudless sky all looked like something out of a fairy tale, or just as easily the scene of a murder. I saw Ricardo, so tense and agitated that I was sure he had already come to blows. His torso was bare, chest and forehead damp with sweat, and his eyes blazed with a violence I had never seen. He was shaking. And brandishing a stick.

Ricardo bashed the stick against the windows and body of the Mercedes and kicked the exhaust pipe and mirrors. All four tires were flat, the hubcaps lay bloated in the dirt. On the ground nearby, I caught the gleam of a knife.

Ricardo's hands were stained with blood, as though he had done hand to hand combat with the car. Sweat bathed his body like he had been doused in oil.

"Motherfucker."

Between insults and threats, Ricardo told me what had happened. It seemed that when his boss found out that Ricardo was accepting tips and exploiting the opportunity to sell his leather goods to the restaurant's patrons, the man had refused to give him the two months' pay he was owed. This was the worst possible outrage: he had stolen Ricardo's sacred time for living, the loss of which was even more painful because it was time he could have spent on the banks of the Fluviá with me, a singular time etched in the Besalú summer.

Infuriated by the con and increasingly agitated despite my attempts to calm him, Ricardo picked up a rock so heavy he had to hold it with two hands. In the glare of the headlights, the black Mercedes suddenly reminded me of an exhausted animal, a panting, savage bull, or shark about to surrender to the harpoon after a long fight. Ricardo raised the rock high above his head and brought it down hard on the front windshield.

He was forced to leave Besalú that very night, like a fugitive. And before he left, he looked at me and made a proposal I didn't hesitate to accept, not even for a second, a question I would have answered the same way even if I had known then that the future that awaited me was twenty years of watching Ricardo locked away in front of a computer. Twenty years of watching him open the mailbox to find another rejection letter, still clinging to the memory of our summer in Besalú, his mock bullfights, and other embellished tales from his Mexican past.

"Guadalupe, do you want to live with me?"

In his voice, I heard his urgency to start the engine, to get far away from there. Even more, perhaps, than his actual question.

∾

We flitted through several towns along the coast, ultimately settling in Lloret. That valet job was the last concession Ricardo would ever make; he never worked for anyone else again. He was done following his mother on her rambling trail, as well; not out of sudden disregard for her feelings, which would have been unlike him, but because she departed for Peru around that time and left him to his own devices on the Continent.

Ricardo was just over thirty, the age when youthful fervor meets maturity, when one has known struggle, and the bitterness of disappointment, but can still have faith that a passionate life is possible. This was the moment in life that he chose to stop roaming and start chiseling his life's work using a modern tool: the computer.

"Like Marcus Aurelius: first the battle, then the meditations." For Ricardo, the move from his past, his whole life story containing its most colorful chapters to date—running contraband in Mexico, drifting through the cafés and bookshops of Barcelona, street vending throughout the Catalonian countryside—to Lloret was itself a feat worth chronicling. At last, he would dedicate himself to the epic canto that would define the sort of hero story he wanted to star in.

By that time, his lungs were already damaged and it wasn't unusual for him to spit up blood, especially when he first woke up or physically exerted himself. His tests results always came back as chronic pneumonia, a result of excesses during his years in Mexico, but Ricardo—with his mordant character and penchant for invoking his romantic status as artist—usually preferred to treat his illness as if it were the very same tuberculosis that killed so many nineteenth-century poets. That, or he boasted about his disease with the same pride of showing off a scar sustained in a swordfight.

"In the past, a man died in armor, on horseback. Nowadays, you have to hide your cigarettes in your pocket or the nurses will confiscate them," he once commented ironically, when I found him holding a blood-soaked handkerchief.

Sometimes his elegiac turns of phrase sounded overblown, especially when he talked about his life from the time he first landed on Spanish soil onward, when he was a young man with literary ambitions who—like many before him—conceded all sorts of random, unromantic jobs. And his hyperbolic descriptions were certainly out of place in Lloret, where his only sorties resulted in unsung victory in city-sponsored writing contests, years of battle waged with envelopes dispatched to towns all over the map: Segovia, Palencia, Jaén, provinces that seemed to exist only so they could hold literary contests for Ricardo to enter, and if his story was chosen from the hundreds submitted by the retirees and housewives hungering after the same prize, he would receive a certificate to hang up in the living room and a check that barely covered half a month's expenses.

It became increasingly difficult—even for him—to keep up the good-humored banter, as if his voice grew thinner and lost its earlier aplomb with the passing of time. In the beginning, humor won out over complaint, his laments were disguised as sarcasm, self-parody fitted over his sadness like a mask, but over time his grievances became darker, and with them the sense that he had been engaging in a decades-long war against no one, a delirium of ghosts on whom he spent all his energy, feinting, striking out at enemies of air and silence.

At times, he was overcome by a terrible intuition that he had wasted his entire life. He made less and less effort to conceal his frustration, even in front of other friends and acquaintances. There was a completely overwrought scene of self-flagellation for not having won a story contest, sitting in tight-lipped silence through an entire dinner with Fernando Vallés. Another day, as he warmed his hands by the heater on one of his usual visits to my office, bearing chocolates or pastries for all, he unwittingly uttered a dark prophecy: "Here he is," he proclaimed, opening his arms and turning toward the desks laden with telephones and computers and folders stuffed with papers, as if he wanted to confess his biggest regrets before all of Lloret. "The posthumous poet."

I would be lying if I said it never occurred to me that I had chosen wrong. I imagined another life with a more conventional man, funny and exuberant but without the insistent martyrdom. I could never stop imagining what the future held for us. There was so little hope then that Ricardo would achieve the success he sought. But I loved him. I believed in him. And I knew that if I chose to stay with him, I must not try to domesticate him. And yet, the pretext that he was taking part in bellic adventures in order to narrate the marvels and horrors of combat afterward was untenable. He became a househusband, nanny, bumbling tutor, second-tier character. A background actor, a kept man supported by the insignificant job I did for us both.

Every morning, as Ricardo got Patricio dressed and fixed his breakfast, I kissed them both goodbye and rushed off to the town hall. If my day ran later than usual, I would come home to find them already immersed in their afternoon routine: Ricardo attending to our son's snack and homework, having done nothing all day but hole up in front of the computer to write books that no one read. In his final years, before *The Aztec* was published and the solitary monologue he'd maintained in Lloret was heard around the world, before his endeavors finally found a massive audience at last, his despondency was so extreme that one day he couldn't even meet Patricio's eye.

Our young son was giving a blow-by-blow account of his school day, from morning circle-time to afternoon recess. They were seated at the kitchen table while Ricardo fed him yogurt.

"Now you go: what did you do today, Papá?

I saw Ricardo crushed by our son's innocence, his tender, unblemished life. His face contorted and he turned to me, the spoon suspended in air, as if it contained deadly venom and he doubted whether or not to give it to Patricio. I knew it pained him to think that he hadn't done anything worth telling his son about. Not that day, or any of the days before. It was the first time I pitied him.

He held my gaze. "Better let your mother explain."

I was dismayed by his desperation, especially when I thought of how exuberant he had been when we met in Besalú. I supported and admired him, of course, and I never doubted his intelligence or the visceral depths of his dedication, but I admit that sometimes I had the impression I was raising him and Patricio both, fretting over whether each one did his chores and dressed and ate as he should.

In the period just prior to the advent of all the recognition and money and readership, Ricardo's only toehold in reality apart from Pasquiano's monthly letters, the only people who validated his status as a writer and confirmed that his authorial identity wasn't simply a figment of his imagination, were Fernando Vallés and Rodolfo García Huertas. Both men were so different from Ricardo: Fernando was an established, prestigious novelist whose books had already been translated into several languages; thanks to his rapid ascent on the literary scene, early on he started to publish articles in *La Vanguardia*, in addition to counting on considerable family wealth. In contrast, Rodolfo García Huertas never harbored the same ambitions as either Ricardo or Vallés: he was content for writing to be little more than a pastime, a Sunday treat, an armchair traveler's fancy.

At the time, I feared that if those threads of friendship were broken, Ricardo would be lost forever in our tourist town, like a satellite escaping its controls and floating off into the infinite darkness of space, where there were no conjectures about the future and where his voice didn't echo and every gesture was a juggling trick performed for an audience of none. Ricardo harbored that same terror, as well.

One afternoon in July, García Huertas came to Lloret with his wife. We were having paella on a restaurant patio, cocooned from reality by the dazzling sunlight and our dark sunglasses and piles of towels and bathing suits and sand pails. Relaxed after two jugs of sangria, Ricardo's old friend from Barcelona decided to make a confession. He wore a red-and-white flowered shirt and had smeared sunscreen all over his face without bothering to rub it in.

"I only write in the office now," he joked, adjusting his straw hat to protect his incipient bald spot from the sun. "Not even that: I just revise the work of professors who need extra income."

He admitted that he was shelving his literary ambitions, mostly because he judged, with chagrin, that his writing wasn't very good, and I couldn't help but wonder what remained of the oaths he and Ricardo had sworn when they met in the Raval, when they traded stolen books and created poetry anthologies and co-authored stories. When neither one of them could imagine a future that wasn't flush with words.

Ricardo already knew that his friend had started working at a press that published textbooks, didactic books designed to organize basic knowledge for schoolchildren, books that were not books as they had conceived of them, despite the paper and ink. García Huertas's admission didn't come as a surprise, but when Ricardo heard it, he gave a bitter smile that neither his sunglasses nor Patricio's presence on his lap could conceal.

Ricardo had on an even more colorful shirt than García Huertas, with daubs of green and blue and yellow, anarchic brushstrokes that seemed to mimic a cockatoo's plumage and a childhood on the Caribbean coast instead of Lima. He took a long drag on his cigarette and seemed to chew the smoke before he exhaled.

"You're doing the right thing," he said, finishing his espresso and getting to his feet. "Maybe it's what we all should do: resign ourselves to correcting other people's work and appreciating it as readers. From a distance."

Sad and solemn as the victim of a sacrifice, a martyr who accepted his fate in the firepit in exchange for the redemption of the very mob that condemned him to death, Ricardo walked toward the sea, in the direction of the little pedal boats. We watched as he and Patricio climbed aboard. From our table on the terrace, we could recognize Ricardo from the back, and the small shape of Patricio on the bench beside him. Ricardo made a beeline from the shore straight out to sea, hell-bent on motoring as fast as his legs could take them, away from the beachfront restaurant and the swath of swimmers at the water's edge, away from García Huertas's admission and the fact that he was down one more companion on his voyage. They were out on the water for close to an hour. We kept watch, unsure if it was another of his half-mad jokes and we should just wait, or if it would be prudent to alert the Coast Guard in case he disappeared over the horizon forever.

એ

Ricardo's acrimonious reaction that day wasn't a capricious, singular episode. There were many other signs. In fact, it was around that time that his despair started to have serious repercussions. Unbeknownst even to me, Ricardo had begun to feel the first tremors of paralysis before his computer. It wouldn't be long before he was incapable of writing at all, having wasted so many words that he no longer discerned the black outline and found himself confronted by a great white flash instead. He was like a blind man faced with the immense landscape of his imagination, whereas before he had always been able to invent great peaks and valleys, whole continents to be shaped and sculpted through the pounding of keys. Ricardo never admitted that he was haunted by the specter of a definitive burnout; that would have been the same as renouncing his name and his past, his being. It would have been suicide, a negation of self so complete that it would have driven him mad. But no matter how he resisted voicing his failure to write, plenty of clues gave him away: if I asked him to show me his latest story, he'd pull up one he'd written years before, or if I flipped through the novel he was working on, I'd notice he had increased the font size and margins to fake a longer manuscript.

One morning, as I left the office to run a few errands, I spied him rowing a little boat in the harbor, shirtless. He failed to mention the maritime expedition later. And one afternoon, I caught him getting off the bus whose route ran along the coastline, for no reason I could think of, and yet another time, I was driving back from Barcelona and there he was, walking alone in an empty field flanking the road. His sporadic excursions seemed to be increasingly frequent, but he never once admitted them to me.

There was one worry I knew I could rule out: that he was seeing other women, which wouldn't have been a problem, even if he had done it every week. Ricardo and I always gave each other the freedom to pursue our fantasies, however and with whomever we wished, without it harming our own relationship. So, I came to an even more painful conclusion, the only one I thought could explain his secrecy: the cellar studio that had been his ideal writing den for years had suddenly become an intolerable prison. I feared that, though he wouldn't admit it like García Huertas had, Ricardo had also given up on his youthful promise. After twenty years devoted to writing, his passion had sputtered out, I thought.

Some evenings, he smelled of the sea, of sweat, of exhaust fumes, not tobacco, and he brought home sand-filled shoes, or pants torn in some hard-to-believe accident, but I didn't force unnecessary explanations from him. The truth was, he slept better after an especially active day.

I intuited that the secret life he wasn't sharing with me was a gasping for air, something he needed to ward off collapse. He was desperate in those days, making a mess of his unpublished manuscripts and removing the story contest plaques from the wall; once, I saw him hurl the culture section right into the trash bin on the street after he'd bought the Sunday paper at the kiosk, sick to death of all the articles and all the reviews and all the literary phenoms.

I never considered leaving him—more because of my accumulated affection than the light he had radiated when I first met him, when his fate shone most surely—but there were times when I was much less concerned about whether or not he would achieve his dreams, but whether his loss of faith would force him over the edge of a cliff. And then, when he was at his most anxious—when I'd begun to consider recruiting Vallés or García Huertas to help him, when his torrential output of words and storylines seemed to have dried up forever and he was teetering on the edge of a black abyss, of jumping out a window or hanging himself in the living room—he got the news of his illness.

It was the great cataclysm: Death had come and it was staying for good. Ricardo had gone to the doctor for a routine checkup. Instead of a new prescription or more admonishments to get in shape, he was met by the threat of a terminal illness. He waited for me at home while Patricio was still in school.

I opened the front door to a sense of doom.

I knew right away that something serious had happened. There was so much smoke that I thought the frying pan had caught fire in the kitchen. But as my eyes adjusted to the murk, I saw it was just Ricardo, puffing on a cigarette in the living room.

He was sitting on a chair in the center of the room, completely naked. To his right, a low table with an ashtray erupting with the stubs of the cigarettes he smoked, one after another, with the windows closed. He sat with one leg crossed over the other, his genitals tucked in the hollow between them; it was a natural position for Ricardo, and one that gave him a sophisticated, feminine air when he spoke. Befitting, perhaps, of an old-fashioned *madrileño* literary salon.

I took in the medallion slung around his neck, his body—as weak as ever, so thin I could see his ribs—his little round clerk's glasses, sparse chest hair, and skinny, untoned limbs, and felt the urge to scoop him up and wrap him in a blanket. He stared up at the ceiling, exhaling a long thread of smoke from the corner of his mouth. He spoke before I could.

"I'm dying."

Just above his head, suspended on a hook that once held a model of a Nazi warplane, hung a miniature plastic skeleton. It was the first time I saw his little toy, white skull and white bones, a scythe in its tiny hands.

The room looked empty of everything except Ricardo and his macabre scene, as if the other furniture and mass of plants and books on our shelves had been spirited away by the smoke, bleached of their solidity by the pearly air. Ricardo remained still, insisting on the abject display of his naked body, the foreshadowing of his shrouded form, of his death, his eyes turned to the light-filled windows and the white façades of the neighboring buildings. I thought about all the meals we had enjoyed at the table in the living room, every breakfast and every coffee and every conversation gone long into the night, all the Sundays he read Pasquiano's poems out loud to me and Patricio, Sunday being the day he reserved to recite the words of his great Mexican friend before he lit them on fire.

Ricardo took another long drag on his cigarette then divulged the diagnosis, a disease of the lungs from which he had very little chance of being saved. He was bitter; he knew he was in for a battery of tests and hospital visits that might not even stave off his impending death. But he had something else, something worse, on his mind.

He waved his hand, gesturing toward the stack of papers that formed another of his novels.

"Maybe it wasn't the cigarettes."

Maybe it had been the days and nights cloistered in his cellar studio, all the lost years, half a life of speaking to a mirror, receiving no response. "It makes sense: if you stick a plant in a dark basement without water and sunlight, it will die, too."

He looked up at the toy skeleton and smiled his peculiar smile, as mad as it was lucid, the absent expression of those who have sought and seen and know too much, and that smile was his way of greeting Death, like it was some whimsical creature, a constant companion until his very last day.

HE WASN'T THE FIRST. There have always been writers whose wastebaskets overflow with drafts of manuscripts, pages riddled with markings and crossed-out lines, until suddenly, as if they had experienced a revelation, as if they had been miraculously given a way to channel their wasted talent, they begin to churn out transcendent, timeless texts. One after another. That is what happened to Ricardo Funes. Seemingly overnight, every word he wrote slid into place with unfailing naturalness. He worked as if touched by some mystical annunciation, though he was merely driven by his disease, conscious that he could no longer squander a single second of his life on another failed paragraph. Everything flowed, every possible meaning of every sentence blooming in the cracks of the page, as if he cut his arm with a knife and stories sprung from his veins with all the authenticity and truth of an ancient, secret stream, no longer willed to the surface by desire but erupting with force of necessity.

Only in his final years did Funes's story—his whole life, really—acquire the coherence of a structured drama, when all the scattered pieces of his biography suddenly locked into place with unanticipated precision. When no one expected it, Funes became the most widely-read and highly-acclaimed author of his generation. Illuminated by the gleam of success, each of his past stumbles was transformed into just one more heroic feat on his sublime odyssey. Funes, I'm sure, could not have conceived of such unanimous applause. Before his star ascended, he seemed to be the only person left who had faith in his talent. I read several of his early novels with the hope of finding sufficient rationale to suggest them to an appropriate editor, but I must confess that I did not see evidence of the brilliance that was later to be revealed—and revered. In fact, his writing seemed to undergo some process of enlightenment: the shaky scaffolding of his texts became straight and sublime, reaching sudden and resounding heights after the publication of *The Aztec*. Guadalupe, for her part, accepted Funes as he had always been. She loved him, not for the prosperity of his last years, but for the conviction and fortitude with which he had resisted the corrosive effects of the preceding decades: "Anybody else who'd spent the time I have with him would feel the same way. To dazzle in youth is less admirable than the ability to wait half a lifetime for it."

☙

Celebrity, however, did not assuage the bitterness he felt about the many years he had spent in solitary, writerly resistance. If he was the personification of a hero, it was a hero of silence and perseverance; if he had somehow managed to elevate himself into brilliance and lucidity, he had done so by first peering into the darkest of depths, the abysses that so transfix those prone to suicide. His case was a perfect example of the perplexing inconsistency success tends to generate in the literary world, as the very people who dismissed him as a madman suddenly venerated him, bestowing upon him a prophet's authority, and the same people who had rejected his manuscripts anticipated every single one of his new books as if they were sacrosanct precepts of a nascent religion.

Another phenomenon was produced almost simultaneously—a common one in such instances and therefore of no surprise to me, as accustomed as I am to the capriciousness of the literary industry: publishers began snapping up his earlier manuscripts, manuscripts that had already been repeatedly rejected, or not even considered at all. It was yet another example of the inconstancy of critics and editors, a class that Funes continued to view with suspicion, even in that most fruitful period. "Pouring your soul into a book is gambling with your legacy, just like roulette," he commented one afternoon as we browsed a Barcelona bookstore where stacks of his books were displayed on the New Titles table, his recent writings consorting with other texts that, for years, had formed his own private, unpublished library. "Maybe you win ten times in a row, or lose every time. A roll of the dice."

While Funes joked about the role of luck in his literary success, I considered the books with their vivid promotional stickers, perplexed: not even I was sure whether for two whole decades his manuscripts had been judged with excessive harshness, shot down for no reason except that their author had never been published, or whether, now that the winds blew in his favor, any old thing he'd ever written would be received with excessive goodwill. I, Fernando Vallés, a writer who wrote about writers and poets and should have had the nose to distinguish real triumph and actual novelty from work bloated with transient popularity, industry flimflam, or any other ephemeral mania, had to agree with him about chance: it is never, ever the same book when received with hands prepared to applaud and pencils poised to underline, versus when the reader knows she's looking at work that no one else has accepted, ready for one awkward paragraph to be the excuse to toss the whole manuscript.

In any case, the important thing was that he got to see success, success that, for Funes, was not defined by attention in the culture section of the Sunday papers or the cardboard cutouts of his silhouette in bookstores, but by the fact that, at long last, he had readers, readers for whom his characters and stories were resurrected from their coffins in his filing cabinets and took on the corporeality and color with which he had always imagined them. He was happy. He enjoyed success, and it allowed him to get out of the languid hermitage of Lloret, as he became a constant fixture at festivals and literary conferences following the publication of *Tráfico DF*, his most-read novel and the book that made him as famous as an author can be in our language, the book that won him all the medals and all the prizes and guaranteed him an armchair in the stuffy living room of posterity that he had always mocked. In just one year, he spent whole weeks in Scotland and Cartagena, or linked flights from London to Milan or Paris; a month didn't pass when he didn't stray from his retreat on the Gironese coast. Suddenly, his life became so fast and active and well-connected that, far from depressing himself with desperate letters that went unanswered and provoked echoes of silence, he was swept up in intense correspondence with writers and translators and critics from around the world.

He was often in the media, promoting a new book or holding court in interviews. On the occasions he was invited to appear on TV or the radio, he spoke with his usual frankness. It amused me to see him refuse to mold his personality even slightly in hopes of getting people to like him: once, during an appearance on a regional TV culture program, Funes became so irritated by a tenured philology professor who, in a show of erudition, made continual references connecting contemporary works with classic texts, that he had no compunction about expressing his opinion in his most aggressive tone: "You, ma'am, confuse the novel with a body to be dissected." He repeated his attacks for the duration of the program, annoyed by every word from that scholar for whom novels were merely pretexts for writing doctoral theses.

❧

Yet amid such cyclonic change, many aspects of his life effectively stayed the same. He kept his home in Lloret de Mar, the old fisherman's house where he had lived throughout his ostracized years, the small rooms where he and Guadalupe and Patricio inched by his collections of Napoleonic army figurines and model warplanes. Not only was he comfortable in his familiar surroundings, but his insistence on staying was also a stalwart defense of what had been his sanctuary. "After the age of thirty, a man is like a tree," he justified, explaining his penchant for sedentarism after a youth spent on the road. Despite his celebrity and economic success, he felt an obligation to the town that had welcomed him as a stranger, and showed Lloret the same loyalty he offered Pasquiano or Guadalupe or his mother.

As for Funes and me, we continued to see each other just as habitually as before. I still went up to Lloret for a breath of clean coastal air when I tired of the traffic and daily grind of the city, although I had to accept that our roles had been reversed: Funes had risen to the stature of Famous Writer and was the one who was in demand, who was recognized everywhere, while I had become the attendant who accompanied the sought-after figure. And the same thing happened with Rodolfo García Huertas, whom

Funes saw just as often and in the same circumstances as always, completely unconcerned that their pastimes might strike some as strange. For Funes, the tenure of their friendship was stronger than the danger of wearing it out.

Funes had plenty of opportunities to demonstrate his impassiveness when faced with the disruptions of fame. I recall a day in Barcelona when, after a discussion we had participated in together at the university, Funes bowed out of lunch with the faculty and left in a hurry. To my surprise, I bumped into him in the Raval late that evening, at an outdoor café across the street from one of the city's few remaining XXX theaters. At the theater's entrance, there were old faded posters announcing movies already out of rotation and an odd assortment of suspiciously broad-shouldered women and solitary-looking men hiding behind the upturned collars of their leather jackets, while at Funes and García Huertas's table the cigarette butts and coffee cups had accumulated after hours of conversation regarding this or that actress's merits. "Her tits were too high, too round," I thought I heard Funes say. He was wearing his old writerly gabardine overcoat. It was autumn and I assumed he'd never bothered to buy anything else over the years. "Fake, they're all fake these days," mused García Huertas, his faithful Catalan associate, who, far from showing any hint of envy, appeared to enjoy his friend's success more than Funes himself.

℃℔

Meanwhile, amid the spate of invitations to universities, and his flights to foreign capitals, Funes's disease progressed unchecked. He never discussed the gravity of his illness with me, nor did he quit smoking, claiming that he had no idea how to breathe without a cigarette between his lips. But Guadalupe kept me apprised of his condition and she didn't hesitate to admit that, if treating disease was a numbers game with unpredictable variables, they hadn't yet landed on the winner. She wasn't holding her breath for a cure. "It would take a miracle," she said.

Despite his doomed prognosis, Funes never lost his sense of humor. One day I visited him in his cellar-studio while he was working on *Tráfico DF*, the novel in which he and Pasquiano had their literary alteregos, and whose plotting served as an excuse to indulge his passion for war strategy: a large map was spread on a table, its geography occupied by toy soldiers—stand-ins for his characters. He greeted me from across the table, a toy skeleton perched atop his head, like a cartoon scuba diver surfacing from the deep wearing a tiny octopus like a hat.

"We should all have a mark like this on our foreheads," he joked, and proceeded to wear the macabre puppet the whole time we were in his studio. I listened as my friend explained the structure of his book, pointing at regions on the map that represented whole chapters, with the uncomfortable sensation that he would be dead before the novel was finished.

Spurred by death's approach, not only did Funes work faster and more efficiently—he was also increasingly conscious of what he considered the inconsequence of his work. It was a contradiction: he was disdainful of literature and spurned the hallowed figure of The Author, no matter how talented, and yet he never stopped writing, not even when he had more than enough money and prestige and less and less time to live.

One afternoon in particular, I saw this contradiction play itself out. We had taken his son to the harbor, where you could watch the fishermen who still fished with their small boats and traditional tack. Patricio was old enough to distinguish which vocations held the most possibilities for excitement, especially the marvelous adventures of the heroes in the stories his father told him. Warmed by the weak sun, we stood beside the black bollards with their coils of rope, watching as Patricio helped a fisherman transfer his catch from the nets to the wooden boxes. It was a peaceful moment, accentuated by the soft sound of water lapping the rocks, and something about it led Funes to give Patricio a piece of advice unlike what most fathers would impart: before he set his sights on becoming a doctor or a lawyer, he wanted his son to try plain, honest labor. Funes was happy writing, even if it pained him that he hadn't lived other lives. Nevertheless, he forbade Patricio from following in his footsteps. It appeared to be one of his greatest worries.

"Avoid pasty-faced men," he said, lifting Patricio up to touch the face of a veteran fisherman, his skin weathered by countless hours under the sun.

Later that day, we climbed up to the Castell d'en Plaja, one of Funes's favorite places to take Patricio and lose himself before the wide Mediterranean views. As we strolled around the castle, Funes spun fantastic yarns of sunken ships and superhuman swimmers and islands bursting with nature, governed by laws that were dictated by the inhabitants themselves. Funes held his son up to the railing so he could contemplate the infinite horizon. "It does exist," he said. "Paradise exists."

I envied him for being a father, then. Funes conveyed the sense that only in the company of a child would the applause that greeted each new book ever cease to be an empty whisper, the flash of a coin dulled quickly in the dust. With children, one could return to the pleasure of stories when the cynicism of age made immersing oneself in them increasingly difficult.

Funes stroked Patricio's hair. "I only write for the money, you know."

I suspected that Funes's exaltation of fatherhood over his vocation as a writer might have had something to do with his own paternal bruises. Funes often recalled how his father had vanished during his early childhood in Peru, only to show up sporadically over the course of his years in Mexico. Such reappearances brought nothing but a repeat of the man's rejection of Funes and his mother, and yet, even as he scorned and resented him, Funes felt they were yoked by an unbreakable bond. Though he hadn't seen the man in decades, when his first novel was published in Spain, Funes sent his father a copy, personally inscribed. Another test of Funes's loyalty: he clung so tightly to his code of honor that he complied even when the allegiance was one-sided.

જ

As Time whisked him toward the end of his life, Funes was ever more prolific, churning out novels and short stories and even publishing an anthology of old poems. He began to say that he was dying, that there was no hope left for him, that soon we'd be able to hang his bones from a lampshade, just like his little plastic skeleton, which materialized dangling from his living room ceiling sometimes, or perched on Funes's shoulder like an organ grinder's monkey. Although his tone was always humorous, Guadalupe confirmed his prognosis was increasingly grim. "Still haven't picked a winning treatment," she told me several months before he died. I never knew what magic spell would have saved him.

And so the accursed day arrived, the day I had long-feared yet knew was inevitable, one Funes had presaged on so many occasions: the day we saw each other for the last time. In the end, our farewell didn't take place in Lloret or Barcelona or even at a hospital, but—unbeknownst to us—just two weeks before his death, over the unassuming hours we spent together at a literary festival in Seville, where we both attended as invited lecturers. It was an invitation I had accepted with delight, a gift for two old friends.

Even though Funes was a most beloved and acclaimed author, one who inspired tremendous reverence, thanks primarily to the legend of his isolation and resistance, I still remembered the day he came—uninvited—to my reading at the bookstore in Barcelona, when he hung around at the back of the store and was snubbed like a stray it was best to avoid.

The scene awaiting him in Seville couldn't have been more different. His event was to be held in the cloister of a historic mansion that had been converted to a cultural center, a privileged space with a veranda and Greek-inspired columns and arches and a fountain of carved stone in the center of the square courtyard. On a red rug stood a wide wooden table, where the panelists sat under ample lighting before the more than fifty people in the audience. A respectable crowd for a literary event.

Funes chain-smoked and took slow sips of water, and though he was joined on the panel by three other writers and a moderator, it was clear that the floor was his. Everyone smiled at him and waited intently for him to speak, as if awaiting the pronouncements of a prophet. Funes rose to the occasion. He didn't hesitate to challenge a fellow panelist, a dull academic who had that very morning given a lecture laden with technical terms and obscure quotes, or savage another conference participant, an Andalusian poet Funes detested because he wrote for various literary magazines with the sole intention of fawning over his contemporaries. "Kiss-ass," Funes declared with characteristic frankness, undaunted by the possibility of the other writers' resentment or revenge, not because he was approaching death and had nothing to lose, but because it was how he had always been.

After holding forth on the current state of Latin American literature and declaring his devotion to a few select writers and his infinite disdain for many others, Ricardo Funes spoke what were to be his last words in public.

The question came from a university student. She must have been about twenty, one of those diligent disciples of language and literature who probably carried around a book of poetry in her purse and admired the men whose books she devoured and underlined, books that kept her up at night, though nobody could hazard a guess as to why, unless they assumed it was because she found the poets very handsome in their jacket photos.

She appeared to have dressed for the occasion, this young woman so interested in Funes's books that she had come to the conference alone. That was the sense I had, at least. With her long brown hair and open-backed green dress and pure Andalusian accent she sensibly didn't try to disguise, she spoke into the microphone, so close that through the rustling of cables and interference, I heard the parting of her lips and the coy exhale when she finished and thanked him, posing the question we had all heard asked and answered hundreds of times: what advice would he, Ricardo Funes—the now-great Ricardo Funes, the man who was read and studied in every country where our language was spoken and some foreign countries, too—give to a young person who had decided to become a writer?

I was sitting just behind her, two rows behind the exposed rectangle of her skin and her perfect shoulders, and I saw how she lifted herself a few centimeters off her chair to hand back the mic, tossing her hair out of habit. The audience waited in silence for Funes's response, and in the pause I noticed that the water trickling in the fountain now sounded with ancient deepness, reminding us that water had existed long before that beautiful building and the presence of all who were gathered there. The air seemed to flutter then: a flicker of night in the lamplight, the flight of a bat—or ghost—no more than a subtle blink of the eye, as if a crack in the nature of reality had opened, and I thought about the absurdity of the roles we all played on that side of the curtain.

Funes saw her. Funes, who was above all else the poet who had embraced life in the Mexican dawn, a man perforated by the gentle murmur of the fountain and the night air and the beauty of all Seville lit up just for him, for his visit just days before dying, the miracle of that theater in the Renaissance mansion and its courtyard awash in orange blossoms, where he had arrived without knowing how or why or for how long. He saw her and he must have felt so tired, so doomed that he couldn't lie:

"Just one thing." He spoke as if directly to her, as if he believed in giving advice for once, as if he wanted her to stay that way forever, as young and sublime as the night, in the green dress she had worn just for him. "Please, don't write. Not a single word."

REGARDLESS OF WHAT THE LAW or religious canons say, every marriage has its own code, a tangle of oaths and hopes and grievances and compensations made of words and habits that can never, ever be judged from the outside.

Our own marriage had one non-negotiable principle: we had to reaffirm our vows each day, without claims of ownership over the other. In this way, ours was a marriage exposed to the elements, constantly in the making, like the structures Ricardo rigged up when he lived as a nomad with his sackful of leather goods, or like his books, which came together to dialogue and argue among themselves, or a house with infinite rooms, where we could hide out whenever and with whomever we wanted.

Our pledge to each other was of mutual acceptance at all times, and we established it from the very beginning, in Besalú, overlooking the elegant Roman bridge spanning the river and the church spires and the rooftops on the worn-brick village houses, all done up for a postcard.

Neither one of us needed, or offered, any sort of profound explanation. Maybe we just sensed that it was the best hope for us to last as long as possible.

A couple of years later, we formalized our commitment with a wedding in a small village in Lleida, where García Huertas's family was from. The village was a ghost town, all but abandoned in the exodus from the rural country-side to the city, and we were already officially married by the time we turned up, Ricardo and I having signed the paperwork before a judge and the two mandatory wit-nesses that morning, but Ricardo's old friend had insisted on flinging open the plaza of his ancestors and playing the part of parish priest himself, assuring us that he knew the best possible place to celebrate the nuptials: the forgotten village's ramshackle church, a chapel built according to rural Roman canon. The roof had caved in from snow, or from a bombing during the war, but no one had bothered to repair or maintain it or even finish tearing it down, and the dirt floor still retained a few stone slabs from the original building. Dry vegetation of the region crept in through the windows and crumbling walls, threatening to turn those ruins into desert brush. No sacrament had been celebrated there in decades.

García Huertas, with his taste for the theatrical arts, presided with the solemnity of a bishop in a cathedral. It was a cold and sunny spring day. The sky shone bright and blue and the guests wore coats and sweaters, but García Huertas donned an orange shawl adorned with gold-embroidered Chinese characters.

He spread his arms wide. He lifted his chin and looked at us and I knew that this solemn but unsanctioned ritual was worth more than whatever we had signed before the judge.

"Ricardo, do you wish to marry Guadalupe?"

Birds were darting in and out through the gaps in the walls, they might have been doves or sparrows or crows that built their nests inside, though later Ricardo would joke that they'd been vultures: we were so still and silent they thought we were dead.

"Every year," he replied, turning to give me an intense look, cigarette between his lips. He was wearing white like a virginal bride, because the truth was that he believed in the sacred power embodied in those kinds of acts. "I want to marry her every year." And perhaps that's what marriage should have always been: perpetual affirmation that yes, I want to share my life with you, not stuffy old vows and a few papers tucked in a folder somewhere. In our case, it was Ricardo who took it upon himself to state that one paramount condition in our relationship.

Those were the terms of our union, from the day I accepted his dinner invitation until the morning of his death twenty years later: every year, every day, every morning, we had to either affirm or renounce our bond, and shoo away the vultures circling overhead.

We lived together for years in a small house that somehow had enough space to find or lose ourselves as we wished. A house with bedrooms and guest rooms where we could escape into solitude, our little home as large as any palace imaginable, and where neither one of us fretted over a stranger's hair on the couch or in whose arms we slept during the siesta.

So, just as I hadn't questioned him about his earlier absences from home, before his first book was published and praised, I didn't ask about the junket that took him out of town once his fame grew, when the invitations and proposals poured in and he was a respected writer and his trips multiplied.

The change had been a drastic one; there were suddenly so many invitations to take part in conferences and festivals, book launches and prize juries, TV interviews and radio programs, with the worst part being that I couldn't go along to all the places he had the chance to see.

He usually called once he was already at his destination, if he was going to be gone a few nights, but sometimes I only knew where he had been once he was back home, when he unpacked his suitcase and surprised me with souvenirs from the places he'd visited. "Wine from Paris," he'd say if he'd been in France, or "Dollies from Moscow," handing me a set of those Russian nesting dolls, or "the Queen Mother's perfume," trotting out a bottle of gin after a flight from London. I knew he wasn't keeping his location secret from me out of jealousy or egotism, even when I only learned the purpose and destination of his trip once he was back with a suitcase full of dirty clothes and anecdotes from some conference or another. Ricardo had always liked keeping up a healthy sense of mystery.

Incidentally, he spent the most time away from Lloret during the same period as his most feverish writing, the months when he was finishing *Tráfico DF* and his words flowed onto the page in tumultuous streams. There were times during that fertile, frenetic span when I didn't even know where he had been or why, and the particular openness of our marriage didn't give me the opportunity to find out.

He wrote the most on the days following his unannounced trips, as if he had mulled over paragraphs on the plane or bus and his characters were puppets that came back full of air and light after exploring a landscape different from Lloret, inflated with the winds of travel and novelty. These were also the days that Ricardo slept best and looked happiest, and it was impossible for me to begrudge his joy.

His sickest years were his best ones. Only then was he able to rule out the possibility that he would have to succumb to a salaried job, as well as avoid the horror of municipal writing contests, that great lottery for aspiring writers that was so hard to bear. Solitary hours in the basement studio were suddenly transformed into a giant open literary conversation, and he was relieved of the insanity induced by writing day after day for no one at all. Yet while the circumstances of his life underwent a radical change, Ricardo himself didn't budge. He kept his usual routines, writing in the unheated basement with the radio playing in the background, drinking herbal tea at his corner table in La Fundamental, and visiting my office, where he would come to share news of the translation of one of his books, or with an opened bottle of champagne to toast some shiny new award. He had stopped grumbling, however: not a single complaint about his inopportune illness. An awareness of death and relief at having escaped the writer's prison of his own making—the pit he threw himself into then spent decades clawing at its mud walls—helped him enjoy every hour he had left to live.

Ivanna's arrival was perhaps the perfect symbol of those fertile years. With the birth of our daughter, Ricardo reached peak satisfaction with his life: Patricio had his little sister and Ricardo could finally say that his family was complete and realized that maybe his disease wasn't bad news after all, because it had warned him that he would die just like everybody else and we had better take full advantage of the brief time we had left together.

The day we brought Ivanna home from the hospital, I lay down on the couch to rest, exhausted by surgeons and midwives and murderous operating-room lights. Ricardo took the baby from her crib and raised her aloft in the middle of the living room like a trophy, while Patricio looked on, fascinated by the spectacle of his father's homegrown beatification. Ricardo held her high in both hands, as if he had finally found a lost child on the beach after searching for hours, or as if we had been living under a curse and that little blonde satellite with crystal-clear eyes, weighing just barely eight pounds and sailing through German bombers and ashtrays overflowing with cigarette butts, was the key to salvation that had long eluded him.

"I did it," he said.

He had finally found happiness.

It was undoubtedly his greatest achievement.

೮೨

But since everything in Ricardo's life was rife with paradox, it was then, when things were going well, when his intimate experience with both failure and success made him more lucid and his writing finally rang with the epic resonance he'd always imagined, when he had published two widely-read, award-winning novels and Ivanna had made it through her first two months of life and he was feeling well enough and there was still some hope for his prognosis, it was then that tragedy struck: Ricardo got the saddest and most unexpected news, the call he never imagined would come and for which there were no words of comfort, the biggest disaster imaginable, the bars of a funeral hymn played on an organ and destroying any illusions he had that perfect happiness was possible for good.

Fernando had come by that evening to go over the outline for Ricardo's grand novel, to hear about his progress and give advice or words of encouragement. When they didn't return from the studio for dinner on time, I went out looking for them.

I didn't have to look very hard. I found Fernando just a few minutes from our doorstep, leaning on the railing on the promenade and contemplating the sea. I called to him, and he raised his arm and pointed toward the end of the beach, to those meteorite-shaped rocks where Ricardo liked to retreat, geological formations that looked like they had been planted there on purpose by some greater force, so that we humans wouldn't forget the violence of the waves and the voracity of the sea in all its indomitable strength.

"Pasquiano is dead."

From where I stood, Ricardo resembled one of his toy soldiers. Motionless at the water's edge, he looked out to sea, challenging the horizon in all its accursed immensity. He had on the khaki gabardine the papers liked to photograph him in, hands buried in his pockets. The dog ran in circles around him, but Ricardo didn't move a muscle. Something apathetic in his bearing suggested a man capable of infinite sadness. He was so alone and so disinterested in anyone rescuing him from his despondency that—knowing his imagination as well as I did—I thought he might get the idea to fill his pockets with stones and wade into the water, try to reach Mexico by way of some undersea passage and emerge with his last breath in that ersatz homeland of his, because the truth was that it was gone now, the only place in the world he referred to when he talked about the possibility of returning to some kind of origin.

The sea was calm that winter day, but hard, as if they were dark waters off the Scottish coast and not the mild Mediterranean. We watched, unsure of what to do but certain Ricardo didn't want us to go to him. Fernando was the one to say it:

"He's the only one left."

And that was it. We stood in place on the promenade while the minutes passed, whole hours even, and watched him observe his solitary wake as the tide rose and rose and he remained as invincibly passive as a statue.

There were people who glanced at him in passing, not daring to speak, but he didn't turn or acknowledge those distant figures in any way, nor did he decamp to a spot higher up on the beach when night fell and there was nothing left to camouflage the monstrousness of the sea, when no light remained on the water except the odd glint from the heavens dancing over the reflections cast by the neon signs of waterfront hotels. Eventually, the tide was up over his shoes—to his knees, even—and Ricardo was just a shape, darker and denser than the night, a bat that had assumed the height and mass of a man. Suddenly, a raucous stir of seagulls exploded beside the rocks, drawn by the cadaver of a fish or some other piece of carrion. *Pasquiano*, Fernando murmured.

In the end, we left him there on his own. I wasn't really afraid he would do something crazy. Or maybe I was just aware that he could drown himself whenever he pleased, that night or any other. In any case, we both knew it was perfectly possible for Ricardo to stand in the water until daybreak, for days even, just as steadfast in his vigil and stubborn in his grief as Pasquiano had been loyal with his punctilious poems.

Ricardo came home in the wee hours of the morning and climbed into bed with his pants on, even though they were soaking wet. Shaking with cold, he lay down but made no attempt to close his eyes, convinced sleep would elude him and battered by a relentless sense of having been orphaned while his mother and father were still alive.

"I've gotten so old," he said.

He had lost his best friend, the man who had been his best friend for a very long time, the man who, for twenty years, had sent one poem every month and helped him survive his long post as amanuensis-in-exile, and duty-bound by the immense debt he owed that friendship, Ricardo would have to cry for him a little each day.

∽

He didn't make a big show of his grief. I rarely heard him speak of his pain, or wallow in his memories of the days he and Pasquiano spent together. He had already told me their best stories many times before.

He did stop traveling as frequently, however, as if Pasquiano's existence on Earth had in some way sparked those mysterious trips, and he combated the emptiness following his friend's death by spending more time at home, with me and his children. I was afraid that—without his pen pal across the Atlantic—Ricardo would fall under the spell of writer's block again, but the opposite proved to be true: he finished *Tráfico DF* in just a couple of months, and the books kept coming after that.

It was strange, really, his commitment to writing: he idolized the adventurer's life, the captains ascending to general for their bravery before the bayonets, the pilots who tallied their dogfighting victories with crosses painted on the backs of their planes, and he hated the gray languor of academia, the churlishness of his fellow scribes parading around with their small literary triumphs, and yet, Ricardo spent hour upon hour in front of his blessed computer, knuckling down on his epic tales of made-up heroes.

Deep down, he felt that writing was really a feeble sort of insurrection. Sometimes, when he was sick of carrying out his subversion-by-pen, convinced of the futility of his books and jealous of the lives lived beyond four walls and a desk, Ricardo would vow not to spend another moment in front of the computer. Of course, he quickly succumbed again to the literary fever that would pursue him until death.

But it was something that had especially pained him during those twenty years he waited to publish, when he sensed that life was like a balloon that was escaping his grip and floating away, lost in the heavens, and he clung to the memories of his months as a black marketeer, exaggerating the dangers he'd faced, aggrandizing his acts of petty-anarchist sabotage as a Negationist poet, just so he could convince himself that he had indeed lived. This was the lesson he was most concerned about teaching his children—Patricio most of all, because at two years old Ivanna was almost too young to really know him when he died. Over the seven years when he was churning out his best books, Ricardo still warned Patricio not to follow in his footsteps. He emphasized the kind of life he thought was best, the kind of life he believed would make his son happiest, a life that—by its very nature—was to be found on the opposite extreme from Ricardo's own, as if he believed his own choices needed special justification.

One August day, when his illness had returned with threatening vengeance and landed him in the hospital for a week, we took advantage of his release and the glorious sunshine and rented a rowboat that could fit the whole family, Patricio and Ivanna acting as stowaways since they were still too little to manage the oars. Ricardo endeavored to row us far from the beach, out to where we rounded a bluff and there was only the sea and stark walls of the coast. The shore was just a few hundred meters away, not enough to produce the dizzying effects of the high seas, but even so, with the yellow strip of sand and roads and buildings out of sight, we might have been in uncharted waters if not for the odd motorboat or modest yacht glimpsed in the distance.

Ricardo put down the oars and turned to me and Patricio, arching his brow and lifting his chin.

"Time to choose," he said, kicking off the game he had devised in which he offered our son two possible futures and Patricio had to choose the most seductive, as if life were a tree and each of its branches presented a destiny to either reject or pursue.

Ricardo proceeded, more solemn than he had been the other times we'd played. Like he had brought us out to that unspoiled place with a secret purpose all along. He stood in the bottom of the boat, legs spread in an attempt to retain balance when every movement seemed to threaten to capsize us. Ivanna sat on the little board across the middle of the dinghy, the most secure spot, while Patricio and I clutched each other at the other end.

Ricardo wore a white shirt, unbuttoned and knotted at the hem, and he had tied a bandana around his head like a shipwrecked sailor in a comic strip. Try as he might to feign the confidence of a veteran sailor, in his round glasses he looked more like a bewildered office-worker plopped in the middle of the desert rather than a seasoned adventurer. Patricio had taken off his T-shirt and left his little torso bare, and, like his father, donned a tattered bandana. With his usual devotion, he paid close attention to Ricardo.

The day was radiant, not a cloud in the sky. The water was a lighter blue than usual. I imagine it now like the emerald waters in a travel brochure, but it's possible that the passing years have gilded my memory of the outing, and our happy family. But there was something I already knew by then: if Patricio looked up to his father as a teacher, as a guide through the mysteries of childhood, to Ricardo, young Patricio represented the prospect of all the lives he hadn't lived, the infinite possibilities of the future-tree, the marvel of exploring an unforeseen destiny down every branch. In Ricardo's teasers of what-might-be, Patricio could peer into the maze of fate, unhindered by debts to the past or frustration with the present: freedom so complete it was impossible to make a mistake.

"Okay," Ricardo said, setting his hands on his hips. "Ship captain or writer?"

Those options presented Patricio with a dilemma: he had to choose between his father's lineage—his father who was, moreover, a kind of recognized hero, a hero of newspapers and books and who, to top it off, played and hunted crabs in tidepools and challenged him in computer games—or the enticing figure of the captain, a man who would see the most exotic places and love women and brave the fiercest storms the world over.

Patricio hesitated.

"Captain," Ricardo said at last, plucking Patricio from the labyrinth of choice and falling backward out of the boat.

He dropped like he'd been shot dead, vanquished by the pull of his bodyweight. He disappeared below for only an instant before he grabbed onto the gunwale and tossed Patricio and me into the great stew of the sea.

We found ourselves treading water a few meters from the vessel, the three of us.

All was calm, as if we had leapt from a perfectly still boat. As if we had suddenly realized that we were actually drifting on a virgin bay in an Indonesian archipelago, and we took off our clothes to bask in the peace of the water and the simple wonder of floating. Ivanna sat motionless on the bench, watching us in surprise and surely wondering what nonsense we were up to, while we observed the little boat with its oars like outstretched arms, barely rocking on the waves.

e/3

It was a very simple notion, really: he would have liked to live all possible lives, explore all the branches of that infinitely-limbed tree, lose himself down every vein of every leaf, play a role in other, distant exploits that he'd only envisaged, not to be contented with just his own.

He would have liked to avail himself of all the possible paths he'd offered Patricio: captain and writer, arms dealer and playwright, journalist and politician and shaman, no single option ever satisfying him completely.

That idea—that he'd only had one chance on Earth, that he'd found himself at a crossroads and taken his own strange way and erred in his direction—was a constant source of pain, the perpetual stab of an arrow in his side, never worse than during that final, desperate period in Lloret when he came to believe that all the words he'd written in the course of his life were so fragile that they would disappear with the next high tide.

Life was escaping him. The days slipped by one after another and there was nothing concrete to grab onto. It was like closing his fist around air: air that flowed where one would have hoped to find solid, lasting bone, air where one would have wished to believe—at the end of the day—that he'd snatched a fistful of fertile earth, reaped a harvest he could be proud of as the shadows fell.

Ricardo was subtle in the expression of his dissatisfaction. When he was already famous and they clamored for interviews on the radio and TV and asked what advice he'd give young writers, what he would do if he were starting over, he would shake his head and speak as if he wished he could turn back on the path he traveled down deeper each day. "I would tell them to live," he'd say, as if he hadn't, and regretted it now.

He was unfair with himself. I thought about how he woke some mornings, impatient to get to his desk and work, or the nights he made a thermos of coffee so as not to interrupt his inspiration, and I knew he had always been passionate and combative in everything he did, that even having been confined to a chair, he never suffered from idleness or indifference.

Yet death arrived before he could shake a sense of guilt that he hadn't drunk life's magic potion to the last drop, not because he hadn't been conscious of the miracle of opening his eyes each morning, but because no matter what he did in life, he would have always felt there was still much left to enjoy.

He died during one of his bad spells, one regular morning in Lloret. There hadn't been any unusual symptoms until he suddenly spoke up and announced that he was taking his leave.

It was an October morning. I remember it was a cold, sunny morning, the kind he liked best because it combined the purity of blue skies with the comfort of woodstoves and warm coats. The two of us were home alone when death's warning sounded, since I had taken time off to care for him after the most recent relapse.

Ricardo was just back from Seville, where he'd bought me a flamenco dancer's fan and a pair of castanets, fascinated as he was by the *peñas'* clandestine magic and seduced by the strangeness of their folklore. He'd had the chance to visit that southern city in the company of his dear friend, Fernando, and seemed happy. Content.

And so there we were—me, busy with laundry and ironing and him recently out of bed, just the unhurried passing of another monotonous morning—when he made a sudden, definitive announcement, the farewell tolling of a bell, and he did it without a hint of urgency, drama, or dread, as if he were simply closing the door behind him on the way out to buy a loaf of bread.

"That's it," I heard him say, and when I followed him to the bathroom, I found the sink full of blood, stained with ghastly vomit.

He was looking at himself in the mirror, more perplexed than frightened, I think, or simply astonished by the strangeness of still standing upright after that deathly retching. Besides the amount of blood flooding the sink, every other detail in the bathroom conveyed a shocking sense of normalcy. Even Ricardo's face: no suggestion of anything amiss except a certain pallor. He was wearing a shirt with blue and white flowers, his hair was curly and mussed and he was rough-shaven. He hadn't showered yet. His glasses no longer helped him see but magnified his sadness instead, his sadness and the absurdity of his face in the mirror, still able to breathe but about to die, a ghost granted leave to take one last stroll before being fitted into the coffin.

The moment had such a peaceful domesticity, such an everydayness, that it was almost irritating that Death had turned up in such a vulgar way before spiriting him off to the void. It was panic-provoking, that stark confrontation with reality, bereft of the daily fictions we'd built to protect ourselves from the madness of the unimaginable: there on the sink, a toothbrush and comb with strands of hair, and Ricardo vomiting again, like he was disgorging his life, his heart, like he had slit his veins and there was nothing to do but witness the lethal draining.

Patricio was at school and Ivanna was at daycare, so maybe it was the desire to spare his children the sight of a dying man's powerlessness, or it might have been the rush of survival instinct or the simple force of habit of responsible citizens trained to seek medical attention in an emergency; whatever our impetus for rushing to the hospital, we chose to perform the farcical act of trying to save him.

But as I cast around for the car keys, Ricardo spoke again.

"Wait, my last novel."

I stood by as he saved the manuscript to a floppy disk and made the final affirmation of his essence as a writer.

So that's what we did: instead of heading directly to the hospital, instead of fighting to hold together the fraying strands of rope that might have bound him to life, we went to his editor to give instructions for the publication of that last novel. His longest book, and the one in which he'd placed his greatest hopes.

The long drive from Lloret to Barcelona, our final trajectory, was like the last dance of our marriage, a farewell waltz, a dance without music or bodies holding each other, just enough movement to keep the hysteria at bay and limit ourselves to remembering how happy we had been together.

I understand now that he must have thought it all through: that trip was our last vacation, the one we'd never take, a few days' getaway to a little Parisian hotel or some quiet town on the coast of Naples, just the two of us. A way to celebrate more than twenty years together before dying.

Naturally, it was his last great comedy. Once we were in the car, in an attempt to alleviate some of the tension, or impart a sense of calm, to seek refuge in the sense of humor that was so him—that soberness and irony, laughter and nostalgia—as if his whole existence had been lived in an attitude of permanent departure, Ricardo began the game we would play the whole way to the publishing house, our final stop.

The game consisted of remembering every year we had been together, one by one, from when we first met in Besalú to our funerary trek to Barcelona, a chronological remembrance that was also instantaneous literature, because when he spoke, he was writing the ephemeral memories he would no longer be able to put on paper, just for me. "Year One of Guadalupe," he said, as I tried to turn the key and start the engine, struggling to inch the car out from between two vehicles boxing us in and avoid hitting a van that didn't bother braking for my maneuver. "The year of swimming under the bridge and promises proclaimed by megaphone."

As I passed through the roundabout and took the high-way on-ramp, as I changed lanes to pass the other cars, he continued his recitation in which recorded time began with our meeting in that village in Girona, just like the ideologues of the French Revolution and their revolutionary calendar, or like the chief of some ancient empire who believed that the world turned by his command. As if I were a myth, and the medieval bridge in Besalú the altar where we had christened our life.

I tried to drive steadily, to accept the seriousness of the situation, but every so often, I laughed. I laughed at Ricardo laughing at death, I laughed because I knew it was the last time I would laugh with him, I laughed because later I would cry for the rest of my life, the life of a lonely or grateful or frustrated or proud widow that awaited me, and as we left the last buildings of Lloret behind and meadows and fields appeared on either side of the highway, he continued his methodical homage to my rule: "Year Four of Guadalupe," he said, and recounted the only time I had ever been spiteful, when I'd been upset by the presence of Swedish students camping a few yards from our tent on the beaches of Valencia. "The year of jealousy and Scandinavian princesses."

We made for the gray channel of the highway, trapped with the drama of death inside our anonymous car, and Ricardo continued the parade of our most memorable chapters, the ones we had always most enjoyed retelling: "Year Six of Guadalupe. The year of nudity and photographers peeping in bushes," referring to an incident that always made us laugh, even though we had been furious at the time.

Once he had covered the first decade of our relationship and we found ourselves in the jammed streets of Barcelona, waiting for a light to turn green, Ricardo lingered on another main event. "Year Twelve of Guadalupe," he said, turning to me with a smile and introducing the year that everything changed and life began again for us both with a happy, drawn-out drum roll: "The gunslinger hits his target: Guadalupe gets pregnant for the first time."

I turned to glance at him occasionally, but he was usually staring into the distance, focused on the empty landscape of the avenue like he was watching the scenery stream past a train window, or the falling rain from his table in La Fundamental, with a look that seemed to reveal the yearning for all he was leaving behind as life moved on, and the discovery of valleys he would never get to explore.

He was wearing his khaki jacket over just a shirt, without a sweater underneath, and he vomited into a plastic bag and cleaned his mouth with a handkerchief. When I placed my hand on his thigh, he patted or squeezed it, as if his plight was worse for me than for him.

We turned down the street where his publisher was located and drove between the stately buildings of the Eixample, lost in the domain of the Catalan bourgeoisie which had—more than anywhere else—always reminded Ricardo that he was the same poor, foreign lover of letters he had been his whole life. He paused, then summoned to mind the arrival of death's black crows: "And in Year

Twenty, it happened: the year of agony and disease," he said, arching his brows and looking at the city skeptically, as if in that solid, noble architecture his dying eyes saw only flimsy cardboard. In a theatrical flourish, Ricardo waved a white handkerchief out the window, a white handkerchief that floated alongside the car like the sails of a Portuguese man-o'-war billowing in the Mediterranean breeze, or like an angel escaping toward the heavens.

I sensed that his antics were the only way for him to exorcise the madness and incurable pain of being alive and knowing that he was about to die, as if he'd wanted to ease the heartbreak of the moment and make a final gesture that would grace his cadaver with a good-natured grimace.

And when I had stopped and parked the car and Ricardo had emptied himself with another spasm into the plastic bag now red with blood, he patted the disk in the pocket of his raincoat and turned to me before we got out onto the street.

His glasses hid his grief.

It had always been easy to make him cry, but that's how it would be for anyone who loved life: anyone who had dreamed of being happy would be pained by how short and splendid life was and how many possible lives one lost each and every day.

"Guadalupe," he said, and reminded me how when we met in Besalú I had told him that I wanted to write a book of poetry, a book with no pretensions of literary greatness, simple notes on life written just for me, to record what I had felt or dreamt in the moment, what hurt me, what I needed, and since then he had always joked that I'd never been able to finish a single line. "Didn't you want to write a book of poems?"

I started to cry. I didn't want him to make that final joke, didn't want to hear his last roar of laughter. I didn't want him to lower the white handkerchief, as though the dove accompanying us had been lost to the sky, leaving me in the car, alone forever.

I put my hand on his leg, as if to beg him to stop, to tell him that I didn't want to hear his last, ironic dig, as he tucked the handkerchief into his pocket.

"Didn't you want to write, Guadalupe?" he insisted, smiling and arching his brow again, both of us conscious that he was about to step onto the sidewalk and disappear forever.

He retched, even worse than before, and struggled for a bit of breath to bid me farewell, a last gasp to celebrate and mourn what he had lived and what he had missed, and to remind me that one day I too would have to get out of the car in those same circumstances:

"Well, you waited too long."

II

I AM RICARDO, RICARDO FUNES. The real Ricardo Funes, since that's what Fernando and Guadalupe have decided to call me, now that I'm dead. They haven't wanted to use my real name, so worn already, like a relic, a fossil.

It isn't important: there are no first names or last names or any other type of identification in death, since there is neither the expectation of the future nor the passionate fury of the present. In death, one speaks with a thin thread of a voice that comes from the distance and filters through the cracks in the void like an inexplicable disaster, smoke slipping through earth shaken by a slumbering volcano.

And so, it is from death that you can talk about the end without hints or nuances and reveal the clean bones of the truth, because now there is no public, no judgment passed on what you say, no other companionship than frank, mute conscience. But at the same time, conscience itself acts as interrogator, insisting on its own questions, the voice that cannot lie once you decide to speak.

Conscience always speaks with the same cruelty, to me and to everyone else, to all of us: if only your life had been different, if only you could cut some episodes short and draw others out, wipe entire years clean and live them differently, though even if we could try over and over, even if life had a rehearsal before it began in earnest on the second or third try, even if we could return to the beginning armed with the wisdom of all the mistakes we were going to make, even then we would still have dark stretches we would want to erase. There would always be regrets, whole catastrophic years, and many other eternally lamentable mistakes, because even the fullest, happiest existence—one that inspires such admiration that a statue is put up after his death and every day dozens of students make the pilgrimage to profess their adoration with candles and flowers and wreaths, for example—even a life like that needs bandages to heal the wounds of the unrealized dreams that haunt us all.

I know this because I know the glory of magazine covers and little bronze statues commemorating some award or another, and because I also know the unease of waking up every morning trapped in the doldrums of permanent doubt. For decades, I faced that peril in Lloret, the coastal town where I ran aground as if I'd reached the very edge of the Earth; I lived assaulted by the terror of having been wrong about my whole life, and I don't mean just one or two twists along the way, but the gross sum of life, unrepeatable and impossible to rectify from death.

I was sold on one idea, having grasped that I wanted life to be a story composed of thrilling chapters for me to relish in some future moment, to recall from the rocking chair of old age. I wanted a story ennobled by the virtue found in beautiful, hopeless causes, and I accepted the danger of poverty or failure or madness over the unbearable hell of conformity. What I didn't know was that in order for my saga to unfold in all its plentitude, for my own personage to reach the dimensions a protagonist in a tale of epic proportions required, the kind of protagonist I'd hoped to be, that in order to acquire the musculature and sinew and haggard profile befitting a man who has accumulated enough wounds and seen enough horrors, I would have to wait so many years and choke down so much disappointment.

It's only from death that I can see, with absolute clarity, the moment I chose the path that was to determine my very existence, and my motives for embarking down that course. Before I even left Mexico, I had chosen the route that years later would lead to my hermitage in Lloret. Lloret, where I would spend half my life.

I was a young man during my most fruitful years in Mexico City, when Pasquiano and I had already organized our web of cigarette manufacturers and street vendors that allowed us to control the tobacco market outside official channels. We had also published an anthology of *negacionista* poets and were so feared for the signs and shouting with which we interrupted poetry recitals and other literary events that we were eventually banned from any venue we showed up at. My time was divided between two antithetical lives; on the one hand, I spent so many hours reading in the library that I could have gabbed about Latin American poetry on the level with scholars twenty or thirty years my senior, while on the other, our activities as tobacco traffickers expanded to such an extent that I had resorted to keeping a knife on me at all times and scoping out the area around the entrance to my building whenever I left the house. It was probably the happiest time in my life, and certainly the one I most enjoyed reminiscing about in the nostalgia of exile. It was also the time that gave me the most material for the fictional reconstructions in my books. And during this period, I found myself forced to consider the seedy character I was shaping up to be against the figure of my father, so I could learn how I wanted to live.

It happened when Pasquiano arranged for me to go to Acapulco—where my father happened to be living at the time—to negotiate with some big Colombian exporters, while he stayed behind to establish new hot spots throughout the colossal sprawl of Mexico City. I headed to the coast to firm up the purchase of several tons of product, obliged to stay with my father for a couple of days in order to conceal my black marketeer's business under the guise of a family visit.

My relationship with him at that time couldn't have been worse. He had left my mother and me years before, before I was even old enough to shave, before I was even a teenager, but for a long time after he would stay with us when he came to Mexico City to oversee some aspect of his murky transportation business, and I still had terrible memories of the shouting that resulted from his continual rifts and reconciliations with my mother, and my feelings with respect to him were an uncomfortable combination of filial duty, rancor for how he jilted and mistreated my mother, and a growing contempt I did my best to conceal.

He lived in a wealthy neighborhood in Acapulco, in a mansion with a yard and pool, and every year he sported a new car and added to his collection of antique motorcycles. He already had a couple of kids with his second wife, a girl who was just a bit older than me and whom I rarely heard speak. In fact, there was such an age difference between them, such coldness in their interactions, and she was so pretty and her features so indigenous, that if it hadn't been for the abolition of slavery centuries before I might have suspected he'd picked her out as a virgin bride in some jungle village.

During dinner, my father drank bottles of beer and watched TV or talked on the phone with his associates, indifferent to the fact that the rest of us heard his conversations, and he had no qualms about counting out stacks of bills on the table either, as if his lust for prancing like a peacock compelled him to behave like that, even inside his own home. I wondered how I had ever admired him as a child.

When they split, I took my mother's side from the beginning; she was a sensitive reader, a peaceful woman who was able to enjoy the simple things in life. In contrast, my father could find no peace, despite his success in business. He had been a boxer in his youth, a Peruvian pugilist with quick feet and a well-aimed hook who gained certain fame on the local circuit in Lima, but before I was born, he hung up his gloves and abandoned his goal of contending for the big world championships. He was convinced that in the States he wouldn't have a chance against the voracious Chicanos and sinewy Puerto Ricans in his weight class, and that it just wasn't worth a smashed nose and blurry vision if he wasn't going to be one of the greats. "You only jump in the ring if you're going to win," he'd told me once, rueful.

Since then, he had dedicated himself to a variety of business schemes, opening and closing bars and jewelry stores, collaborating with construction companies in need of trusted men on the jobsite, until he left Peru for Mexico and founded the first commercial transport line to connect Acapulco with the capital and, in time, became a rich and powerful man.

Each year his business grew and he acquired new trucks and bigger warehouses and made more influential contacts. He wore expensive clothes and necklaces, and watches of silver and gold, he put on weight while maintaining a hearty complexion and, as he advanced into his fifties, his voice became increasingly deeper.

It stood to reason that he was embarrassed by me, the only child from his first marriage; I represented a link to his past, to a previous life he now repudiated, and physically and spiritually I could not have been more different from him. "The blue bard," he scoffed when he read my first poems. I assume he intended to make me feel ridiculous enough to look for more practical ways to keep myself busy.

He had no idea that I bought and sold tons of tobacco, though I'm sure he took note of my material independence despite the lack of evidence that I had a steady job, and he might have even suspected that I too had learned how to pass stacks of cash under the table. When I mentioned that I had to go to Puerto Marqués—the exotic, touristy bay dotted with new beachfront developments, finished hotels interspersed with empty, crane-studded lots—to take care of an outstanding debt, he foisted his presence on me.

"Well, would you look at that, we're frequenting the same places now: maybe our tastes have more in common than you think," he said. As luck would have it, he informed me, he also had to be in Puerto Marqués the following night. He offered to book me a hotel room so we could spend the day together. "Just like when I took you to the beach as a kid. Only back then you didn't have that long hair and a cigarette hanging out of your mouth all day."

He barely glanced at me as he spoke, taking his eyes off the TV for a mere fraction of a second, as if his offer was a natural command I couldn't decline. We were in the middle of the after-dinner domestic lull: my father in his leather armchair and his wife on a corner of the couch, as inscrutable as if she were wearing a mask. Under the cheerless glow of the big screen, she looked pierced by a terrible sadness and I imagined that sometimes the blood of her ancestors must have stirred within her, nostalgia for the exuberant possibilities of another life instead of being trapped in a prison of television sets and swimming pools.

Apparently, my father and I were treading the same road, he with his gelled hair and metal-buckled, patent leather boots and me in my worn alpargatas, both obliged to deal with similar business associates. It was the first time our feet had ever pointed in the same direction. My father, who in my view was one of the most abhorrent individuals imaginable, a man as unhappy with his second wife as his first, a man who proclaimed for myriad excuses why he hadn't fought for his future as a boxer, a man who seemingly preferred a couch besmirched by indolence to a past he could have been proud of. A man who dyed his hair, both to cover his graying strands and conceal his dirty old soul. A man who, whether he admitted it or not, was somebody who lived life continually grasping for the unattainable fiction of the future, the phantom of change, prosperity that would never be enough. A man who, even when he commanded the largest, most powerful fleet of trucks in all of Mexico—maybe all of Latin America—would never believe their number sufficed.

"Okay," I said. We turned back to the variety show on TV. "I just want to check out the bay."

We were both lying, of course, and neither planned to divulge his criminal activities to the other. The charade was a mutually-accepted pact of pretense, at its heart a reflection of the essence of our relationship.

In any case, the next day we made the drive to Puerto Marqués in his new white sports car. I only needed a few minutes outside the hotel to carry out my assignment. It was a typical street-corner deal, down an alley lined with dumpsters brimming with stones and bags of cement and other building materials, and I went straight back to the luxury resort my father had booked, to my room with the double bed and big-screen TV and view of the pool. From my window, I could see the Pacific stretching into the distance, where its monstrous waves crouched, poised to gather and pounce and deliver a fatal blow.

For his part, my father didn't bother trying to keep up appearances, even with me present. He was staying in the company of a young woman with bright, bleached-blonde hair who was outfitted in fishnets and a sequined dress. He'd had no compunction about reserving a room right next to mine. As a consequence, I had to spend the whole duration of the siesta trying to ignore the squeak of the bedsprings and pounding of the headboard through our adjoining wall. But the girl's companionship must have been so dull, her permanently sour look—despite the new coat, the new purse—so insufferable, that after dinner my father sent her back to the room, and he and I were left alone.

We sat on the outdoor patio, a few meters from the edge of the pool ringed with empty glass tables and wicker chairs. The whole night unfurled before the two of us, uninterrupted except by the waiter who came around every few minutes.

My father was drinking champagne, a bottle he stored in a metal ice bucket. His face was tanned and freshly shaven, and with his unbuttoned shirt and silver bracelets, he looked like a man on a permanent summer vacation. As he emptied the bottle into his long-stemmed glass, I sipped tea and smoked one cigarette after another.

"You're just drinking that dirty water to fuck with me," he joked, one of his sporadic attempts to connect with me, affronted by his son's delicate habits. In his mind, the only possible sign of my virility was my penchant for cigarettes.

He hadn't raised me, except for the anodyne period of early childhood, and it had been a long time since he provided my mother and me with any kind of material support, but he gave himself license to dish out advice whenever he felt like it, whether it be mounting an attack against writing poetry or arguing about other practical matters. In an attempt to steer me down the right path, he talked about the satisfaction he got from his big house, and the money he had for trips and hotels and countless nights picking up the tab, round after round, the gilded dream of wealth and comfort that seduced so many and made him so unhappy.

All of a sudden, he seemed to tire of my disinterest in the conversation he was directing at me from across the glass tabletop, and stood up.

"I'll be right back. I'm going for cigarettes," he said, winking at me as he counted out a stack of bills so ostentatiously that his little ruse was stripped of any cachet of danger.

I acknowledged his announcement with a nod and drank the last of my tea. I watched as my father skirted the pool and crossed the area where empty hammocks swayed against each other in the breeze. Then, he disappeared behind a row of palm trees that stood like skeletons in the penumbra, crucified by the wind blowing off the ocean, their fronds tossed about by the mass of dark air that was like liquid ash and seemed to stir at the same time every evening, only to return later, calmed, to its dominions.

It was a gentle wind, perfectly synchronized with the steady tempo of the waves as if by some act of magic, as if wind and water joined forces in the deepest fathoms and set out together on their subtle march to conquer the coast. As I contemplated the setting, I was suddenly struck by the feeling that, with its dense vegetation and vigilant, hulking mountains, the whole bay emanated such impenetrable lushness and mystery that it wasn't out of the question to imagine menace springing from any corner.

I got up from the table and walked to the side of the pool, leaning over to find my reflection on its surface. I was sporting my characteristic style: a leather hat set low on my brow like a gaucho or detective, ripped jeans, and an open shirt, so rawboned that I imagined somebody taking me for a recently released convict, or a kid who'd lost his soul to the needle. Who was I? There were as many hypotheses as the mind could conjure up: my face was a blurred impression, a watery likeness distorted by excessively bright patio lights, as if I were a man yet to be defined, his outline only roughly sketched. And yet, I recall thinking that the portrait cast in the aquatic mirror did in fact resemble who I aspired to be at the time.

In an excessive architectural flourish, the pool had been built in the shape of a palm tree, and its position as centerpiece of the hotel felt just as garish as the gigantic TV in my room. A tall line of hedges stood as protection from the ocean, suggesting that refuge could be taken in that thoroughly silent hotel. It looked exactly like the set of a gangster movie. It occurred to me in a flash that all that was missing were the gunshots and blood splatter clouding the water.

Just then the waiter appeared.

He was a young man whose face, like that of my father's second wife, conserved the indigenous features of the area's first inhabitants: very thick black hair and a broad, flat nose. He was short and compactly muscular. The white uniform jacket and little black bow-tie didn't favor him at all.

In a voice so soft it might have been a veiled warning, he asked if I wanted more tea.

"No thanks," I replied.

Only when I spoke did I realize how long my father had been gone, and I thought of him, a Peruvian who had landed on those shores in order to build his luxury chalet in the best part of the province, a conquistador who—instead of razing the population with swords and arquebuses—had come to dominate the populace with his trucking empire. I had a vision of the ancient caciques delivering justice with bloodshed.

That was when I turned and saw the palms buckling in the wind, as if the night was about to strangle them, and they seemed to me to warn of the brutality lurking beyond the boundaries of the hotel, the wildness of the ocean and the wind that the locals had coexisted with for centuries and centuries, and, spurred by that ominous premonition, I went out to find him.

I wasn't wrong to think he had been gone too long. I might never have seen my father alive again if it hadn't been for the waiter's inspired intervention.

I recognized his silhouette as soon as I stepped off the hotel property and onto the beach. He was about a hundred meters away, at the shoreline, beyond the reach of the hotel's lights, out of sight from the promenade and road that ran along the bay.

Actually, I could distinguish three figures. Two shadows loomed near my father, the space between them the precise distance of rival gangs poised to do battle, as if the beach was a wide, open-air alley, flanked by mountains instead of tall concrete buildings. *Peruvian piece of shit.* One of the waylayers had a strong Mexican accent. My father's heavy form took a few stumbling steps backward.

I sensed the attack was about to begin and that the roar of the ocean and the murky night fog were the perfect cover to conceal the crime, and I knew that despite all of our differences, he would always be my father and I his son, that I owed him the gift of life, and blood.

I drew my knife.

The night sky was muddled by a scattering of clouds and the light pollution from Puerto Marqués barely grazed that part of the beach. I must have looked threatening as I advanced toward them, with my lean, mangy mien, like a starving greyhound, the knife gleaming in my hand, a lunatic with nothing to lose, more inclined to kill someone than recite a poem.

"Leave him."

My voice sounded with unexpected authority, more an affirmation for my father than a threat directed at the strangers.

My command convinced them, and the two shadows backed away, never turning their backs on us, uttering invectives and threats, expressions of their fear and the need to create a barrier to protect them until they reached a safe distance. My blade saw no action except to shine, unsheathed, like a sword that cast the spell to bring peace to the land once and for all. There was no violence that night, save that of the waves.

Back at the hotel, I'd already put the key in the door to my room when my father took me by the shoulders in a gesture that was an acceptance of his ruin, of his defeat. He had been a boxer afraid to enter the fray, and he used stacks of bills to buy the dignity he didn't defend in the ring. His expression was terrifying; for a moment he seemed to search my face for his reflection, a common interest, a parallel between us.

"You want to be partners?" he asked.

I experienced a revelation in that very instant: my contraband network would grow until it became as big as his fleet of trucks, and what happened to my father and boxing would happen to me with poetry. Lured by money and complacency, I would abandon writing and choose success over adventure, survival over risky pursuits.

I shuddered.

When I returned to Mexico City, I abandoned the tobacco business. A month later, I took off with my mother for Spain.

એ

For years, I felt the same confidence, the same predilection for crime or death, as that night in Acapulco. Far from renouncing the oath I swore before the slumbering Pacific, I was happy in the precariousness of exile, poor but convinced of the dignity I shouldered, certain that dropping anchor in Barcelona added both opportunity and exoticism to the story I aspired to live.

And so the years passed, one after another, ever faster and ever the same, ever leaner in feats and adventures to record in my thinning journals, until one day the tranquility of Lloret, the months of empty seafront streets, the excess of hours and days with nothing to occupy my time aside from the scribbles on interminable blank pages, became my worst nightmare.

It had been so long since I abandoned Mexico City and the extralegal tobacco business, so long since I left Barcelona and its bookstores and cafés, so long since the traveling flea markets took me all over Catalonia's interior. Those parts of my life were so far in the past that it was impossible to do them justice, to express them in the present, and I had the sense that I was suffering the revenge of fate, like a bureaucrat descending into madness on the Russian steppe, waiting for messages that would never come.

Eventually, the flow of words dried up. After what felt like eons of writing and revising drafts of manuscripts then organizing them in folders and drawers, I was paralyzed. I believed my whole life could serve as a parable for a giant mistake: I had tried to live an epic, frenetic life, but my story went off-script and now there was nothing but blank chapter after blank chapter in which the only plot was an increasingly frayed nostalgia for a time so far in the past that it could have been a mirage.

There were days when I was sure I'd gone crazy, a madman talking to himself in a white, padded room, a failure whose words fell on deaf ears, when all along he had claimed that he came to this world to shake it with his roar.

I couldn't believe in my own work. I wrote novels and

stories filled with young people proclaiming their intense love of life, adolescent poets fervidly roaming the streets of Mexico City, its outskirts and its most luxurious neighborhoods, prophets whose only commandment was to renounce all forms of cynicism and cowardice, young people like I had been once, long ago and for such a brief time. If I had intuited back then that I would become an aging scribe with habits best described as vegetative, I would have despised myself.

But the truth is, I never wanted to write about anything else. I never wanted to write books about tedious lawyers or dissatisfied husbands or corrupt politicians, much less books about disillusioned writers. I wanted to write books about characters who raised themselves up as heroes, like statues on horseback, sabers drawn and pointing in life's true direction, the models I hoped would ultimately inspire my children.

So one day, I simply stopped. I went mute, hands hovering, tormented, over the keyboard because I simply could not write another sentence about those figures sailing their ships to uncharted territories when I myself was holed up in a port, frightened at the first sign of the battering seas. My computer screen became a blinding flash, the very mirror of my own blindness, a clean, dry absence, and every time I went across to my basement studio it was like handing myself over at a dungeon to have my arms and legs shackled and submit to the torture of one-sided conversations I no longer expected would have any impact whatsoever.

I started slipping away from my desk during the day, playing hooky from my writing schedule—self-imposed and strictly kept—embarking on escapades that Guadalupe must have had some inkling of, of course, though she would never say a word or be so imprudent as to investigate. We had a pact to preserve our privacy and she respected it, despite the fact that I was using my freedom to shroud myself in mystery for the worst reason, betraying myself in the most infantile act of cowardice, spurning the life I enjoyed in Lloret and each and every one of the years that had led me to that spot on the coast, never revealing my conviction that I'd made a terrible mistake.

I sought the amusements of a man of leisure, the sorties of an unfaithful husband or recalcitrant teen averse to the demands of the school day, amusements that weren't actual opportunities for pleasure but mere excuses to escape my prison.

They were survival strategies: a drowning man gasping to get a bit of air in his lungs. Sometimes I took the train to Barcelona, for example, alert to the scenery through the window and my status as a perpetual spectator, and visited an old lover who had gotten in touch with me after decades, a woman for whom my company was the novelty that helped her survive her numbing home life. And in that contemplative, anticipatory state in which I found myself, I wound up accepting the proposition from a former waitress at La Fundamental, a Chinese woman who was a little older than me, big-boned and not very attractive, after numerous invitations to her house in the countryside a few kilometers outside Lloret. Her property could be accessed through fields used for crops and livestock, which I preferred to cross on foot. It's better this way, I told her when she offered to take me back by car, it's like Aesop's fable of the farmer and widow. The extra time and effort required for the walk home weren't a problem, but part of the relief I sought.

Oftentimes my plans were less original, trips to Barcelona just to talk with Fernando, or lose myself with Rodolfo down the streets we had frequented as young men. I felt less and less like talking about books I had read or my plans for novels. I was tired of a whole life spent behind the curtain of fiction. I even lost interest in pornos. Fernando came to see me sometimes, but I sensed condescension in his attempts to lift my spirits, and there were even occasions when I suspected that Guadalupe—increasingly concerned by my obvious isolation—had asked him to come see me.

And so, short on other enticements and apathetic about my oldest pastimes, I developed a new strategy for evading my studio, setting out in the rented boats powered by pedals rather than oars; Patricio's favorite boats, incidentally, partly because of the boy's fondness for bicycles and partly because—like his father—he was more coordinated when it came to his feet than his arms.

In any case, those sham fishing trips became a happy routine. Even if I didn't shove off abuzz with a spirit of adventure—I was fully aware there was no more bravery in those ebb tide incursions than a naughty child's escapades—at least my little secret ignited a flame in which I found a bit of peace.

Every morning, after wishing Guadalupe a good day and dropping Patricio at school, I headed in the direction of the harbor. When I turned toward the sea promenade and away from my basement office and took in the empty beach and calm waters, I felt the immense joy of being alive. I had finally given myself license to rest after decades of unremitting work.

I often pedaled straight out to sea without a compass or fixed destination, determining my location by using the coastline as reference. Other days, I was inspired to take along my fishing pole, even though I released any fish I caught back into the water, alive and unharmed except for the brief panic of capture. When I got tired of pedaling, I would swim, nude, careful not to lose my rental boat, and on the hottest days, I took off my T-shirt and tied it to the fishing pole, raised behind me like a mast and flag. After a few outings, I resolved the issue of how not to contaminate the sea with ash and cigarette butts by hanging a plastic sand pail from the side of the boat.

The days when I went out, I returned home soothed by the elemental pleasures of sun and sea, contented by the simple fact that my body was fatigued and my lungs clear after breathing the free sea air, and asking myself why it had taken me twenty years to indulge in that simple luxury.

One day, I pedaled several kilometers away from Lloret along the coast until I came across a rocky outcrop and decided to go ashore. I tied up the boat with a quick knot, then took a short swim and caught a pailful of crabs. Spent and satisfied, I lay down on a flat rock to catch my breath after the exercise and playing a game of cat and mouse with the crustaceans that scurried among the rocks' nooks and crannies. I did nothing for several minutes, just lay naked on my back, clothes tucked safely in the boat so they wouldn't get wet, and watched the high, clear sky and the vanishing contrail of an invisible airplane. I smoked a cigarette, holding the pack and lighter in my other hand. My lungs would get no break.

But not even in that peaceful moment could I escape the thoughts that had been pursuing me for months. By then, I knew that my circumstances weren't solely to blame for the emptiness of my days, to my internment in the basement in Lloret where I faced the mute blinking of the computer screen. I had realized that no matter what I did with my life, no matter what path I chose, it would have never seemed enough. I could have lived the life of a Napoleonic dragoon or champion boxer or of a poet laureate read by young people as impassioned as I'd once been, and still I would have been assaulted by the sense that my time skittered away without sufficient substance. Any feat, any victory or immolation, any act of heroism right out of Greek mythology, was too small, too skimpy, if what you wanted was to live out your ephemeral existence in a state of constant exhilaration.

Nowhere, absolutely nowhere, could I have found the unfailingly intense life I'd craved, no matter the turns I took in the labyrinth of my then forty years—there simply was not room for the kind of lasting ecstasy I professed in my Negationist manifestos in Mexico City, except perhaps in Pasquiano's poems, which burned as they were read.

I was absorbed in those thoughts, having smoked three cigarettes lit one after another from the burning ember, diligently saving the butts in the pail-cum-maritime ashtray, when I sat up and looked on the expanse of sea and saw that my boat had gotten loose and drifted several hundred meters from where I sat on the rocks.

"Shit!" The craft was just a yellow smudge, already farther away than I'd ever swum before.

Naked, cigarette dangling between my lips, I accepted the fact that in order to get back to Lloret, I was going to have to submit to the shame of walking to the nearest town and calling Guadalupe, a disoriented nudist.

The boat bobbed on the current, moving farther out to sea. I watched from my perch, pained by all the days that had passed one after another and never left a single memorable mark, a single scratch, like pages blown about by the wind, which no one can quite manage to read. And in that instant, I found myself confronted with a secret opportunity for heroism.

It wasn't unlike what I had faced in Acapulco decades earlier, really, pulling that knife on two strangers on an isolated beach, where I could have easily wound up drowned in the night ocean with no motive for such a suicidal move other than a sense of duty my father would never have toward me.

I tossed the finished cigarette into the beach pail and carefully picked my way down the jagged rocks, then dove in and started to swim. I didn't know whether or not I would reach the boat, if I would get ahold of it and pedal myself back to Lloret, or if I would be forced to wave my arms around and shout for help, having risked, by my own volition, a fortuitous rescue by a couple of fishermen.

As I swam under the sun and felt my lungs strain with the effort and the tobacco and the disease that was already consuming me, it dawned on me that there were two ways to confront the succession of my dead calm days: I could give in to the safety and inappreciable stream of blank pages, or I could rush ahead without a life jacket to be imperiled by writing and the temptations of suicide.

❧

Who doesn't know what we all know from the moment we are born: that you will feel the premature hands of Death tighten around your neck much earlier than you imagine, that the days and years pass with increasing speed, as if instead of a parceling out of equal portions of time, each portion propelled the next, a whirling vortex gaining strength from inertia, so that the final stretch of your life becomes but a brief interval that ends in a flash of dust? It's something like that, something like that, they tell us, those who came before we were ever conscious of being. No one questions this as truth. And when they diagnosed my disease and that diagnosis turned over the hourglass and I experienced all of my remaining breaths falling grain by grain, I had a reason not to fail. It was the dynamite that finally blew up the dam that had held back my torrents of fury and frustration and vestigial hope like nothing else.

That was when I came up with *The Aztec*. I wrote it in scarcely twenty days, hardly stopping to shower or drink coffee, more likely to eat standing up than at a table. I didn't even want to go across the street to Guadalupe and Patricio; I swore to return back home only when I was completely clean, once I had expelled every trace of sludge and spewed it into a dying man's final missive, because if that novel had failed, then I would have smashed the computer and never written another sentence. I either kill this or blow my brains out, I told Guadalupe, as if I were locked in battle with some kind of monster only I could see, a circumstance which bore some relation to the plot of the book itself: there was a character, who, after a long stint as a fugitive, emerges from darkness and stands in the light and consummates his revenge for his past in poverty and exile. It was me, a repudiation of my life as the only way to accept it. I was convinced that someone who had emerged from a well as deep as mine was more capable than another man of enjoying the same wisp of wind or ray of sunlight.

During that time, as I got sicker while my books conquered storefronts and shelves, after I got notice of my death and felt more alive than ever, something unexpected happened.

Pasquiano telephoned.

I'm here, he said, and I no longer sensed the thousands of miles of the Atlantic Ocean between us: Pasquiano had arrived on an impromptu trip to Europe, as if he had long hidden a secret desire to visit the most important capital cities with their big rivers and gothic cathedrals and graves of the writers he most admired.

Just like that, I started spending more time away from Lloret, partly because of all the invitations to literary events—where I'd gone from being a nobody to enjoying a permanent seat at the table—but sometimes because of Pasquiano's phone calls. Throughout his months-long European tour, my friend would abruptly summon me to the most unlikely places. I never revealed to Guadalupe exactly where I was going; to me, the rendezvous with my old friend belonged to a sphere as intimate as if I'd shacked up in a hotel for a few hours with a woman.

Even for Guadalupe, who had listened to my stories for years, Pasquiano's presence would have proved disconcerting. Most people, in fact, would have found Pasquiano's behavior incomprehensible: just as he burned his poems, he frequently scrapped one way of life only to initiate another, the result being that one never knew where he was living or what he was up to. His purpose didn't align with anyone else's: after quitting the tobacco trade, he became interested in the virtues of plant medicine in southern Mexico, in the jungles of Chiapas, and then moved to Ciudad Juárez to run a cantina with his wife, only to return to Mexico City to set up a distillery producing traditional liquor that he sold in bottles with folk adages printed on the label.

This big trip to Europe was his latest gambit. I had no idea what he had done with his family or how he was supporting himself. He had no planned itinerary or particular intention, enthused, I suppose, by how close the cities were to one another. The best way I could host him on that foreign continent was to wait for the phone to ring.

I tagged along every time I had the chance to during those months. He would call, out of the blue, and invite me to join him in London, in Edinburgh, to go see the home-turned-museum of some great national poet, and I would head almost directly to the airport, because I hadn't seen him in decades and I missed him. With Guadalupe, I used the pretext of some literary event or obligation related to the translation of one of my novels, regardless of how implausible the explanation.

She surely suspected that I was maintaining a parallel life, but she was happy to see me happy. Meanwhile, I considered my newly honed skill of packing a suitcase at a moment's notice as a pale version of the uncertainty with which Pasquiano operated; for my friend, the next day would also constitute an absolute question mark.

I met him in Geneva, Paris, and Trieste, destinations chosen for their literary mythology. I was struck by the fact that Pasquiano never took pictures or bought a postcard. In terms of my own role in our jaunts, what excited me most was how we recouped the delirious rhythm of our time in Mexico, when we never knew exactly what day it was, when for months on end I spent more time awake at night than during the day, when publishing with a big press wasn't an option or a concern or a dream remotely comparable to the pleasure we took in handing out fanzines and artisanally stapled magazines.

"Miss it," Pasquiano would dare me when I was already on my way to catch the return flight to Barcelona. He was as tall and tranquil and thin as a preacher, sure and slow when he spoke, gifted with a sense of humor so serious that practically no one could tell whether he was joking or not.

There were times when Pasquiano's erratic trajectory took him from Germany to Portugal, or Ireland to Greece, and I had no way of getting in touch with him. That's when I wrote *Tráfico DF*, a novel nourished by the memory of our past and enriched with scenes plucked from our latest travels. Just as Pasquiano didn't separate the past or future from the present, I didn't set boundaries between real and imagined events.

The novel was an exaggeration of my youthful adventures in Mexico and subsequent nomadism in Spain, adventures in which Pasquiano shared a starring role in their mythical recreation. I wrote us both, emphasizing the characteristics that defined us: Domingo appears as the paradigmatic hero, audacious and full of life, while I personified the man bound by his calling as writer, a man whose greatest merit lay in his finely tuned capacity for observation.

The truth was, I had always been more high-strung, more of a con man than my friend. I had traveled more and known more women, but I had long since realized that the number of anecdotes one can tell isn't what defines a character's essential spirit. The reason I wrote Pasquiano as a warrior with feats worthy of being sung, a man who launched off down the most uncertain paths and spurned mere contemplation, was because he had always been capable of living firmly in the present. He scorned any calculus based on the future or posterity, as exemplified by the poems he wanted destroyed as they were read.

It was, perhaps, the greatest difference between him and my father: while one aspired to expand his fleet of trucks and build a marble pool in the backyard and have a reserved table in all his usual restaurants, Pasquiano came to Europe with no planned purpose or prospect for earning money, on a trip so precipitous that he may well have dreamt it up the day before he left.

I wrote more—and better than ever—during Pasquiano's stint in Europe, as if my imagination were a stream that swelled thanks to surprising tributaries in which my oldest memories ran alongside more immediate experiences, and whenever Fernando Vallés came to Lloret to observe my progress on *Tráfico DF*, he was astonished by the rapid expansion of the map I used to plot the action and the scattered toy soldiers standing in for people from my past. *You must have a ghostwriter in here*, Fernando said, incredulous.

It was one of the many miracles of that time: though the clock hands ticked at the same pace, it was somehow possible between one breath and the next to accrue many more experiences than before. The days transformed into infinite plains, into whole lives with hermetic compartments waiting to be filled with indelible chapters, and I never spent more time with Patricio and Guadalupe and Ivanna than I did then. In that state of bliss, I could only wonder how other years had slipped by like wisps of smoke, indistinguishable from one another. For decades, I had been accumulating layers of sediment in Lloret, and now the time I had left was tumbling toward the precipice with the unstoppable force of a landslide.

Eventually, following stops in various capitals, Pasquiano touched down in Barcelona, where he informed me that he'd only set aside one morning before he would head for Madrid.

"Madrid is the capital," was all he said when I met him at the airport, as if what mattered was Madrid's administrative clout. I couldn't tell whether he was teasing me, or whether he lived in such a state of self-absorption that it was like his rationales came from another planet.

Not even the fact that we were pressed for time could persuade him to tour the city in a logical way. On the contrary, he spent the few hours he did have searching second-hand bookstores for magazines in which some of his old poems had been published, just so he could buy and destroy them with a pyromaniac's zeal, compelling us to rove from one end of Barcelona to the other instead of visiting the main sights, all due to some baffling ideas about his writing: *To disseminate is to diminish* is all he would say. Eschewing grandiose references to silence or the pure passion of the present, he simply tossed his old poems into the trash after shredding them to pieces.

I never understood Domingo, despite the fact that he was always my best friend. I simply accepted and loved and admired him as he was, and it was in this capacity that I joined him for the trip to Madrid, still uncertain of how—with such divergent literary trajectories—he and I turned out to be the only two members left of a movement that wouldn't have existed if not for our promise of eternal loyalty.

In any case, after tossing a stack of magazines into an open shipping container and dispatching them to their origins across the Atlantic by barge, a return trip that was a kind of atonement before the burning that awaited them at a garbage plant in Mexico, the time came for him to depart for Madrid. It would be the last city Pasquiano would visit before we said goodbye and he flew back to Mexico City.

We eventually abandoned the train to continue Pasquiano's proposed route by bus. Once we had passed Zaragoza, we opted for a regular route that ran through several of the province's interior districts, a stretch requiring several bus changes and stops in village after village.

So it was that we arrived purely by chance in Monegros, a semi-desert whose topography was completely unlike well-known Saharan expanses, with their kilometer after kilometer of fine sand dunes, immense and golden, instead, it was an arid wasteland, dotted with brush and tall rock formations whittled by the wind, terrain that had never been home to pastures or cropland. Its desolate scenery—devoid of the cacti and infinite horizons of Mexican deserts, blessed with nothing but lonely roads and the odd village weighed down by the poverty of its surroundings. It was, to Pasquiano's eyes, perfect.

"Paradise," he said.

He hustled me off the bus, as if he had espied the distant sea after a long pilgrimage, weary of the crowds and clamor he'd tolerated in Europe's grandest cities, I supposed.

For a moment, I committed the mistake of trying to decipher his thoughts, imagining that perhaps Pasquiano meant such a place was the best possible environment for him: after all, in the desert, nobody did anything for applause or posterity or melodrama, and he himself never acted except in accordance with the genuine impulse of the present moment. Still, it might have been nothing but a quip, his humor undetectable in the seriousness with which he always spoke, or it very well could have been that Pasquiano's aesthetic proclivities simply didn't jibe with the majority and the gray plateau with secondary highways like stitches seemed as marvelous to him as the discovery of a cascade in a virgin jungle.

Whatever the case, the bus drove off and he and I were left in the village, which only had a few years left before the tides of rural depopulation would carry its inhabitants off once and for all. The only sign of hope was that the rural highway ran through the center of town. My first thought was to wonder how we would get out of there, a concern I already knew Pasquiano didn't share. He looked around him, attentive to every detail of the prototypical village in the Spanish heartland. There was a bar, a simple establishment with a metal counter and metal stools, a single patron just barely visible through the open door. Clusters of terraced houses were heaped on a knoll at the base of the hillside. Each building was constructed using the same basic architecture: two storeys, façade finished with a rough layer of concrete.

It was hard to get our bearings, to know whether we could reach a larger settlement by walking north or south, east or west, adrift in the wilds of ravines and dry riverbeds, monotonous if not for the beauty of a few rocks the wind had worn down into statuesque shapes. We headed a few meters down the single road leading out of town, the village behind us. We soon came across empty plastic bottles and cast-off bathtubs and cracked sinks, the outskirts of town turned into a dump. The desolate sight of steel-lattice towers and electrical cables strung across the plain only served to underscore the isolation the region's inhabitants would have suffered before the invention of the telephone.

It was impossible for me to know what Pasquiano was thinking. He was dressed in a black suit-coat and pants, bald, hatless, so tall and so thin that he looked like a caricature of an alien. It never bothered him that he looked strange, nor did he ever attempt to use his odd appearance to get attention. He had never worried about whether or not I liked his poetry, and in several decades of friendship, he never once voiced an opinion about my work.

"Wait here," he said. He stepped off the road. "I'm going to read."

I stood on the shoulder and watched as he tromped off in the direction of a promontory soaring above the arid plain. The eroded rock formation was shaped like a tower or turret, a geological phenomenon common to Los Mone-gros, a small-scale replica of the great stone peaks that rose in the American West. Pasquiano reached its base after a few hundred meters, then started his ascent to the top of the elevation. He looked like a shepherd, or a shaman cloaked in black. A messiah come to announce the way to the sea. To freedom.

It is one of the very last images I have of him alive: raised upon the rock like a scarecrow defying the wind, head bent over a piece of paper. We were alone, the solemnity of silent prayer blanketing the desert. Pasquiano's last reading, the last of his readings that I would ever witness, because next came Madrid and then Mexico and then two months later I would get word of his death.

Everyone who knew him always took him for a madman, someone who loped around, anesthetized by drugs or medication or some accident that had left him isolated in his own world, and maybe that's who he was, but for me, it was impossible not to admire him at moments like that. He must have carried those verses around in his pocket for days, for weeks, all so he could read them when he felt moved to do so, held aloft in the wind that lashed the Spanish steppe.

❧

His death came without warning. There were no prior complaints, no foreshadowing of danger. He was killed unexpectedly in a traffic accident in Mexico City. A bus mowed him down as he waited at a crosswalk for the light to turn green.

The details came by way of an anonymous letter sent, perhaps, by an old Negationist associate unwilling to identify himself for shame of admitting his betrayal. When I read the funereal note, I didn't consider drowning myself or crossing the ocean on foot, but I did—for the first time in my life—grasp the terrible vacuum of orphanhood, the mad fact that we are exposed to the great, unbounded mirror of the universe night after night. As I stood on the sands of the beach in Lloret, the water up to my knees and my feet numb with cold, I repeated to myself that each and every human is condemned to wage a battle that is beyond us. A battle, it occurred to me as I thought of a Napoleonic army's endless ranks, that was like a single carabiniere sent on orders to defeat an entire armada alone.

But not even Pasquiano's death would alter the whirlwind pace at which I was writing at the time. The prognosis for my disease was as pessimistic as ever, and since I had no youthful vows or debts of loyalty to the ghost of my

Mexican friend and was conscious that death numbered my days with Patricio and Ivanna and Guadalupe, I took refuge in new plots and new novels.

I sometimes told myself that I wrote out of a pressing need for money, but there was no such need, and Guadalupe would never have allowed me to hide behind that excuse anyway, given that she kept her job at the town hall. In the end, I reached a surprising conclusion: that after my stint as a peddler with no compass, stock, or fortune but survival, and my subsequent hermitage in Lloret, where I'd suffered pangs of conscience for having misspent my life, in my quest for a life worthy of posterity, *writing*, it seemed, suddenly presented itself as the way to finally be a man of action.

A paradox, then. The paradox of letters made weapons, words made bayonets with which to pierce the page and exact revenge against my own destiny, which I had judged—until then—to be so harsh. Even when, in my very last days, I conceded to forgo the practice of sitting at the computer, even when I still believed some of my best days had evaporated unbeknownst to me, the fact that I had maintained a steady hand for decades—to the point of becoming a genuine pariah—cast me as a heroic resistor parapeted in his fortress until fate struck with belated success.

I accepted this conclusion in order to keep writing as I waited for death, producing in seven years an oeuvre equal to a prolific writer's lifetime and never cheating Patricio or Ivanna out of a single hour with me. My only regret was that I hadn't become a father sooner, so I could have played with them unencumbered by the fatigue of illness. And as for Guadalupe, the woman who had watched me grow old and never complained that I had dragged her into my strange life, I knew no one else would have had such patience and faith in me, and realized that my belief in my work was owed in part to her confidence.

I decided on a second wedding as a way to celebrate how fate allowed us to find each other in all the world's enormity, in Besalú, twenty years earlier. A mock ceremony, of course, because the papers were already signed and we made no changes to the easy contract that had always ruled our union. But instead of a crumbling chapel in an abandoned village and a decent number of friends ready for a party and music and wine, the second time around was an intimate affair on the cliffs beside the Castell d'en Plaja. I put on a black tie and white shirt and Guadalupe wore a dress and heels and a flower crown, while Patricio donned a sailor's cap and Ivanna a gown the same shade of sky blue as her mother's.

As if it could have been any other way, after a day at the beach, a shorts- and sunglass-clad García Huertas reprised his role as officiant for our improvised rite. He teased me for my insistence on ceremoniousness, as if we were traditional country bumpkins more conventional than was to be believed, peasants who not only prayed over the sowing of seeds but also at harvest time. *But it's true*, he said, resting his hand on Patricio's shoulder and holding Ivanna in his other arm. *You've had a good crop.*

That was it, essentially an excuse to take a picture on the balcony overlooking the sea. Evidence that we had been a happy family.

She and I lived a whole life together, united by a promise so fragile that, on any given morning, either one of us could have shaken our head and the knot between us would have unraveled. Neither one of us ever turned away, though we may have enjoyed our own private trysts that were never divulged. I assumed she had, surely, even if I never went sniffing for strange cologne on her clothes or secrets in her diary, and that's as it should have been, since there was no way to ensure that she would return to the bed we shared other than to leave the doors and the windows open and wait for her to decide where and with whom she wanted to sleep. As for me, in spite of my self-exile in the basement studio and my anemic scribe-in-thrall-to-his-runes pallor, I continued opportunities for the forays that served as a distraction, and I enjoyed them—not only for the novelty of a new body, but because I inhaled each one of those episodes like air to later breathe into my books.

Many of those women were conquests that lasted for months. Others, I saw only once.

The woman I visited most, during the early years in Lloret, was a veterinarian I met when I accompanied García Huertas to the clinic with his injured dog. She worked there, and as soon as I saw her clean and wrap the animal's paw and administer medicine on its long German Shepherd tongue, I felt a flash, as if I held up a lantern whose beam suddenly illuminated the face I'd been unknowingly seeking in the immensity of night.

It was a mutual revelation.

"Send me those books," she said. I was already suffering from seduction's venom, the impossibility of thinking about anything other than her.

For several months, I saw her every week at her secluded house near Sant Cugat, where she lived an old-fashioned villager's life. The only thing missing was for her to wash her clothes in the river and balance a milk jug on her head. She spent over an hour on her daily trek to Barcelona because she liked to be surrounded by greenery and enjoy the company of animals. She preferred to light a fire in the hearth instead of turning on the gas heater. Every time I entered her home, there were so many cats and dogs underfoot that I never knew which ones actually belonged to her and which ones had snuck in, looking for warmth and food. She grew all manner of plants on her parcel of land and tended her own vegetables in a small greenhouse.

She was pretty, a Scandinavian kind of beauty, blonde and blue-eyed with freckles that gave her a youthful look, but her most striking feature was a prosthetic leg, the left one, which she had lost due to a horseback riding accident as a teenager. She walked with a slight limp and when she took off her clothes and removed the prosthesis, I found myself in bed with a new kind of intimacy. I was conscious of the hollow concealed under her clothes every time I slept with her, and as we tussled in the sheets, I felt that for a few moments I was saving her body from an irremediable orphanhood, as if it was the missing leg that had condemned her to spinsterhood in that remote village, as if she had accepted infinite retreat and solitude as the amputation's consequence and made do with the crumbs of my fleeting companionship.

She never complained, never reproached me or asked questions or pushed herself into my life as a married man. Her only concern was which day I planned to visit, so she could fix me a salad with the large, misshapen tomatoes from her garden, or give me jars of jam, which I in turn gave to Guadalupe under the pretext that I'd gotten them from the owners of La Fundamental.

She was the woman I had spent the most time with, apart from Guadalupe, and I cursed life when she returned to Andalucía to care for her sick mother, waving to me for the last time from her doorway, as if we were in the Swiss Alps and she had taken me in as a lost soldier in wartime. I would have liked to go with her, if it hadn't been renouncing familial contentment in Lloret.

"Write," she told me.

That was my wedding ring, and Guadalupe's, too: we were allowed to keep the windows open in order to let in a new breeze from another neighborhood or city or country, to invite whoever we wanted to come inside, or slip out ourselves, if we felt the temptation; there were never any bars or blinds to impede the flow of fresh air, because for us there was no greater horror than turning one's own home into a prison. Yet, our intention to live with the one rule of committing to one another with every new sunrise did carry with it an inevitable risk, of course: at some point, one of us might not come back.

I had felt that fear shortly after I met Guadalupe, when during our stay at a campground in Cadaqués, she had preferred to sleep in the protection of another man's arms for a few days, a kid her own age, young and athletic. The guy had long hair and a beard, and made me feel scrawnier than ever.

We spotted the intruder for the first time together on a September morning. We were lying in the grass beside our tent, a few meters from the beach. He was the only person brave enough to take on the chill of the sunless day and enter the water, where he performed his daily laps, swimming out to sea and then parallel along the coast. I made the mistake of commenting on his display of manliness before the harsh elements. *A bushman*, I joked, imitating a monkey. We watched him from our spot near the beach, as he dove repeatedly under the waves and the rest of us went for our sweaters and blankets.

We would later learn that he was also a rock climber and worked as a beginner's guide on the local mountains, and that his discipline with swimming and other sports was owed to his dream of being a PE teacher. He had a remarkably good nature. If new guests at the campground struggled with setting up, whether because of inexperience or because the ground was uneven or for any other reason, he would help them pitch their tents or bring rocks or lend them the right ropes, and if someone's car wouldn't start one morning, he leapt at the chance to find the cables to jump it.

With his appetite for community spirit, he made paellas for dozens of people and shared his watermelon and wine whenever he had extra. Before long, he seemed to know everybody at the campground.

On top of it all, he often lit a bonfire outside the tent where he slept near a group of friends and offered a free juggling show, tossing balls and sticks into the air and breathing fire from his mouth, tricks he'd learned in his past as a street performer. It was September, so he could still brave the night's chill by the fire, half undressed in colorful striped pants, shirtless, like a witch doctor, and those of us on nearby sites would gather around the fire while he performed his acrobatic spectacle, throwing the balls while simultaneously crouching on the ground, or launching into a handstand and doing a dance, his whole body inverted and supported by just his arms.

One of those nights, I saw that Guadalupe was hypnotized by his performance, a revealing smile and gleam in her eye. I watched the other man and knew she admired him for his broad, sweaty chest; he was some kind of fire god, a manifestation of strength and beauty my poems were powerless against. *You don't get a body like that lifting books*, I whispered in an attempt to disparage him, but Guadalupe replied with annoyance, fed up with how I resorted to irony when faced with the simple fact of the juggler's physical dominance.

It was spite on my part, clearly, because the truth was that my books of poetry were losing their weight. And, finally, the inevitable happened: for two nights, Guadalupe didn't return to our campsite. I watched the dawn light through the tent fabric, sleepless, in hopes she would decide to come back, since the pact of our alliance permitted her to sleep on whatever scrap of land she wanted to. Upon discovering that I'd become a sentinel awaiting her elusive ghost, and faced with the impossibility of rivaling the hunky rock climber, I opted for the only solution:

"I'm leaving," I told her, without the demands or reproaches or dramatics of someone who felt he was owed. I trusted only that the nights we'd held each other on the dolmen in Besalú were powerful enough to provoke an attack of nostalgia.

And in the weeks that followed, I took no action but to send her postcards from the towns and villages along my defeated lover's journey, the sad retreat of a hangdog poet, of a downcast troubadour with his flutes and guitars, useless against a warrior's armor and resentful of the hours I'd spent with books and notebooks instead of building muscle in the sea.

I traveled from fair to fair in the various coastal communities from Girona to Tarragona, with stops in Sitges and Salou, villages I observed with the emotional distance of a dying man, removed from the groups of effusive foreign tourists and the relaxed families, absorbed in my penury as a solitary Peruvian with a backpack full of papers that nobody wanted to read. I planted my leather-goods stall beside the other carnies offering plastic hats and candy; I sold very little, so little that as I progressed southward, my pouch of savings shrunk instead of expanded. And for as long as those ruinous wanderings lasted, I did nothing to convince Guadalupe to come back, since I knew that to badger her was the wrong approach, more apt for a husband who considers his patrimonial rights guaranteed. I had no weapon to claim space in her memory except the postcards on which I informed her of my whereabouts and entertained her with superficial anecdotes to try and camouflage my inconsolable pain.

I cried and despaired and hated literature more than ever—even more so than during my agony in Lloret, when I choked on the mute sputter of my words—and I didn't compose a single verse, not one bitter or ragged line. I was always more prolific when in an exalted as opposed to dejected state. And on it went until one night, on the boardwalk in a town I couldn't even distinguish among the number of towns I'd passed through, all subjugated to the permanent pulse of the August heat and crowds, I ran into a group of local teens riled up on booze—the kids insulted my Peruvian roots, to which I responded with suicidal imprudence. *White piece of shit*, I said to the first one to step toward me, for which they threw me to the ground and kicked and punched me until they wore themselves out.

I wound up with a busted lip and black eye, scrapes on my hands and knees, and a bruise on my back that left me incapable of lying down for several days.

But when the punches stopped mattering, when I couldn't have cared less about taking a worse beating and getting tossed like a package into the sea and drowning below the waves, when I went days without eating and cared so little about how I looked that my hair started to fall out, when I was fully aware that until my dying day, nobody, nobody but Guadalupe would ever understand me and the desperation I felt as a spurned lover rendered the mere idea of future happiness absolutely impossible, an answer to one of my postcards arrived, and it arrived with the same terms upon which we had forged our alliance, with no excuse or explanation, but vibrating with real joy at being together again: *Where should we meet?* she wrote. I was on my way to Lloret de Mar, a town I'd never set foot in but whose name on the map suddenly sounded like the right place to settle down.

❧

A short time after the second wedding, the fake wedding in the shadow of Lloret's famous medieval-style castle, my disease began to show irreversible symptoms and my options for survival were reduced to the miracle of an unlikely scientific discovery. Those were the circumstances when I received the invitation to lecture in Seville, which I happily accepted, because I would be going with Fernando Vallés and the idea sparkled with a promise of warmth and vitality and fiery music in the midst of doom.

It was to be my public farewell, the last event where I would speak, and the last time I would leave Lloret before going to the hospital to die.

And on the last night, at a roundtable organized in an old royal mansion, a building built in accordance with the Renaissance architectural canon, including semicircular arches and Greek-style columns, as well as a fountain with Mozarabic influences, a young woman posed a question that unsettled me.

I had been asked the same question hundreds of times, but that time I knew that my lungs were as full of fluid as a ship about to sink and that girl's apparition, that angel from another world who had come to show me the exit, could not have wounded a dying man more deeply:

"What would you tell someone who wanted to write?" She spoke into the microphone, so shyly, so sweetly, that I felt the tremendous pain of the hours I had spent before a piece of paper, the days I had wanted to live but didn't know how, the wonders—like her—that had passed before my eyes and which I didn't appreciate as unrepeatable miracles, and the sadness of every minute that slipped away while one dithered over the path they should take, or how they should move their arms to catch the wonder of life, more difficult to hold onto with each passing moment.

As I looked her in the eye and answered with greater concentration than if I were standing before a painting or landscape, I had the sudden thought that the unbidden young woman should have never learned to read or write or maybe even speak, that she should have remained—naked and young—somewhere where civilization's poison would never reach.

Seeing her in the audience in her green dress, her arms and back exposed, shining among the dozens of already aging men and women, speaking with a timidity and innocence that collapsed all my readings and categorical statements, so far removed from me that I couldn't even grasp how we could both be alive at the same time, I thought that there was nothing to fear if eternity was like that, beauty so simple and frank, as fragile as glass you hesitated to touch. All I had read and all I had said over the course of my life bored me and the mere fact that I had been sitting at the table and speaking in front of her for so long made me miserable.

The idyllic setting lent itself to that kind of exaggerated reflection. The soft spring night, words almost whispered before an intimate public, the lateness of the hour and the steady gurgling of the fountain and the lights all created a propitious atmosphere for grand confessions, like a couple dining by candlelight.

That was how I explained it to Fernando, who had sat behind the girl the entire discussion, so close that he boasted about the smell of her perfume and the nervousness he had detected in how she crossed and uncrossed her legs before speaking.

"Now I can die," I declared hours later in mock exaggeration, swearing that I would renounce all my awards and accolades for just one night with a young woman like her.

We were in a tavern decorated with the most awful Sevillian folklore, the walls papered in tiny prints of suffering virgins and photographs of flamenco legends, Spanish guitars, and bulls' heads behind the bar, an atmosphere that leaned heavily on the Andalusian stereotype sought by tourists. Taken in by all that imposed authenticity, Vallés was trying a drink called the Blood of Christ, a name that suited the terrible taste of a mix of hard liquor and excessive sugar served with a flourish in a deep red glass.

It was already well into the night and there we were, the two of us, seated at a table inlaid with green and white tiles, beside a signed portrait of a long-dead bullfighter, flipping through the books we'd been given by our writer colleagues, none of which we considered reading. Tired of so much literature and so much protocol, Vallés kept insisting on the excitement with which the young woman had watched me throughout the whole event.

We had decided that, based on her age and the devotion with which she spoke to me, as well as the fact that she had come alone to a lecture dominated by a middle-aged audience, that the admiring young woman must have been an aspiring poet.

"Imagine if she dropped her folder and we could read her verses: I'm sure there'd be one dedicated to the great Ricardo Funes," Fernando said. He blamed me for not taking advantage of her interest to invite her along to the tavern.

A familiar scene, then: two men of a certain age, beguiled by the fantasies youthful beauty ignites, and we knew from the number of books we had read and films we had seen that we had little choice but to accept the rather dishonorable role we were playing.

We were old and nearsighted, Fernando practically gone bald and me with a few thinning patches, our wrinkled skin pocked with hundreds of disappointments and each of us of crammed with pills to keep us alive another day, but still Vallés amused himself with the very thought of the young *Sevillana* reading our books in her room at night, captivated, unaware that we would have fallen at her feet before she'd even said a word.

As he waxed poetic about erotic fantasies made even more embarrassing by the age difference, Vallés alluded to specific passages in my novels, one in which a pair of twin sisters swap lovers in the garden shed on the family estate, for example, or a story in which a prostitute seeks out married men upon whom she enacts her revenge for an infidelity, or the amorous sufferings of a young poetess obsessed with a prestigious male writer. *That's how you seduced her*, Fernando joked, even though we both knew that we were tired of the body's desires and it wasn't the spark of sexual attraction that had provoked us, but nostalgia, pure and simple, nostalgia for female beauty that had always been an unsurpassable wonder and—in recent times—the cruelest and most obvious expression of the life that had slipped away.

A most eloquent way to face the melancholy of time, I thought, so eloquent that I wanted to weep for the magnitude of the missed connection: while we looked at her, fascinated by something so far removed from us as her perfect face, she, in contrast, was interested in us for something as absurd as our books.

I drained the last of my chamomile tea. I already sensed the imminent flood of blood to my lungs, the clot that would kill me in a matter of days, and certain I would never return to Seville and that the student in the open-backed green dress had represented a parting gift, I patted my jacket in search of the document I'd been keeping for some time. Pasquiano's last poem, the one he had given me at the airport in Madrid four years before, about to depart for Mexico City, never to return. He had handed it to me with the knowledge that when I decided to read it, to burn it, his voice would be extinguished as well. "It really is the last one," Pasquiano told me as he said goodbye, assuring me that he would write no more poems following that European tour, that he had found his happiness in silence and withdrawal, that it wouldn't be long until he would achieve his dream of becoming a jellyfish afloat on the waves, surrendered to the pleasures of light and water sliding over his body.

I smiled to myself. After four years of waiting, the time had come to open the envelope safely stashed in my pocket for so long.

"I'll be right back," I said. "I'll see if I can find the girl so you can give her one of your books, too."

I left the tavern and found myself in the sort of narrow Sevillian street designed for taking a postcard photo or painting a folkloric scene, the houses with their lattice-grilled balconies brimming with bright flowerpots, white-painted buildings no more than a few stories high, and I imagined the old swashbuckling days, when men would have dueled and died and killed each other, bloodied by daggers in alleys just like that one.

A place to either kill or die, I thought, and roused by the thought, I carried on with my own knifing and Pasquiano's too, our joint journey into silence, because together we had known the thrill of literary subterfuge and the traffic of contraband tobacco and together we had plotted to keep our conspiracy alive, with no purpose other than simply giving ourselves to the guerrilla war against nothingness, and I knew then that very soon I, too, would dissolve with my friend into the blankness of the extinguished flame.

I read his poem to myself, but under my breath, because I felt that perhaps I had to speak the words to honor his memory, even if my voice was nothing but the thinnest thread, and as I read, I thought how what I had before me was the same poem as always, the same poem we had written, he and I, the same poem that thousands and thousands of poets had written over the centuries and would write until the end of time: verses that celebrated the free and fierce life, the uncharted life in which there could be no defeat, unless it was the failure of the man who removed his gloves before the bell signaled the start of the fight.

He had expressed all of that in his usual way, without bold gestures or dramatics, a voice so flat it was neither poetic nor beautiful, not even in the humblest search for simplicity, a succession of lines in which I wouldn't have found any unique value if it hadn't been my friend Pasquiano who gave them to me before he got on the plane that would carry him to his death.

Before I went back inside to Fernando, I stood under a streetlight whose dim flicker cast the folded page with the hue of ancient parchment, of papyrus that might reveal the secrets of the pyramids or the truths of a lost civilization. I tasted bloody reflux in my mouth, the early sign of the vomit I would expel weeks later in Lloret, with Guadalupe. I reread the title of Pasquiano's posthumous poem: "Last Words on Earth," he had called it, a flight of fancy that foretold a journey, a state of bereavement, of solitary navigation through the infinite expanse of the universe.

I did it, then. I took out my lighter and lit the page, I lit it and didn't let go. I held the edge of paper between my fingertips, and as it burned the flame grew and grew so rapidly that the cremation lasted no longer than the blink of an eye, just long enough for the tiny bonfire to briefly illuminate that corner of the no-name street, until what was left was so insubstantial that it wasn't worth suffering the sting of the flames, just to hold it a few more seconds in my hands.

JAVIER SERENA was born in Pamplona, Spain in 1982. He has published *Las torres de El Carpio*, *La estación baldía*, *Last Words on Earth*, and *Atila* (forthcoming from Open Letter). He has stayed at writers residences with the Fundación Antonio Gala (Córdoba, Spain) and Les Rècollets (Paris, France).

KATIE WHITTEMORE is graduate of the University of NH (BA), Cambridge University (M.Phil), and Middlebury College (MA), and was a 2018 Bread Loaf Translators Conference participant. Her work has appeared or is forthcoming in *Two Lines*, *The Arkansas International*, *The Common Online*, *Gulf Coast Magazine Online*, *The Los Angeles Review*, *The Brooklyn Rail*, and *InTranslation*. Current projects include novels by Spanish authors Sara Mesa, Javier Serena, Aliocha Coll, Aroa Moreno Durán, Nuria Labari, Katixa Agirre, and Juan Gómez Bárcena.